HIDDEN GRACE

A NED FLYNN CRIME THRILLER

MATH BIRD

MCSNOWELL BOOKS

Copyright © 2022 by Math Bird

All rights reserved.

This book is a work of fiction. Names, characters, places, and incidents are the product of the author's imagination or are used fictitiously, and any resemblance to actual events, places or persons, living or dead, is entirely coincidental.

No part of this book may be reproduced in any form or by any electronic or mechanical means, including information storage and retrieval systems, without written permission from the author, except for the use of brief quotations in a book review.

For Yan.

HIDDEN GRACE

A NED FLYNN CRIME THRILLER

MATH BIRD

PART I

1

The police had detained him for ninety-three hours and still couldn't prove a thing. Ned Flynn's involvement with John Mason's death remained a mystery, and anything linking him to Ronnie boy's disappearance was circumstantial. What use was an anonymous tip-off? As Flynn's lawyer pointed out, *they were grasping at straws; it was their word against his.*

Flynn had been in and out of prison enough times to know the score. He kept his story consistent. Mason had hired him to find his estranged wife, Nia. Flynn and Nia had hit it off and had been a couple until she ran out on him.

'And what about John Mason's death?' asked DI Taylor.

Flynn shrugged. 'What about it?'

'Were you aware of it?'

'How couldn't I be? It was in all the local papers.'

'And Mrs Mason mentioned it?'

'Course she did. She was his wife, for God's sake. She attended the funeral.'

'Was she upset?'

'Yeah, considering.'

'Considering what?'

'That he didn't treat her very well. He was a mean-spirited man by all accounts.'

'And you didn't like that?'

Flynn leaned back in his chair. 'Before my time, nothing to do with me. I'm not the jealous type. I never dwell on a woman's past.'

'That's hard to believe, Ned. Surely you had words with him.'

Flynn and his lawyer exchanged glances. 'Nope,' Flynn said. 'We talked when I first took on the job. A few phone calls, perhaps. But after Nia and I became a thing, we never spoke.'

'And why is that?'

'Why do you think? I had no need. Never gave him a second thought until Nia went to his funeral.'

'You didn't like that?'

'Like's got nothing to do with it. It was Nia's business. It was up to her if she wanted to pay her respects.'

DI Taylor released a deep, exasperated sigh. 'And Nia Mason can corroborate that?'

'I guess.'

'And where is she now?'

Flynn shrugged. 'Your guess is as good as mine. Like I said before, she ran out on me.'

'Did you go after her?'

Flynn shook his head. 'It never crossed my mind. I had my own troubles to worry about.'

DI Taylor nodded. 'Your mother's illness.' He regarded Flynn for a moment. 'Does the name Martin Haines mean anything to you?'

Flynn shook his head, his face impassive as his heart pounded in his throat.

'Come off it,' DI Taylor scoffed. 'Nia Mason must have mentioned him.'

Flynn released a heavy sigh, but before he could utter another word, his lawyer interjected. 'Detective Inspector Taylor, Mrs Flynn died just before my client was taken into custody. Both you and I know you've no evidence against him. You can't detain him much longer. Mr Flynn needs to mourn. The poor man needs to arrange his mother's funeral.'

~

LOOKING DOWN AT HIS MOTHER, lying in the Chapel of Rest, was the saddest thing Flynn had seen. Her face was gaunt and pale, a deflated mask with the life sucked out of it. The image would stay with him forever. Yet knowing that she died alone would haunt him most. Nia and Haines were to blame for that. It wasn't just about the money now. They were the reason Flynn's mother died without her son to hold her hand. The reason she took her last breath in a ward full of strangers.

With wet eyes, Flynn stared down at his hands. He'd hound them without rest, force them to make amends, although deceit as costly as this was beyond redemption.

'Are you all right, Mr Flynn?' said the voice behind him. 'Take all the time you need. This must be very difficult for you.'

Flynn turned to meet the lanky, immaculately groomed undertaker standing before him. A detached coldness lingered in the man's eyes, affirming that, for him, death was all too familiar.

Flynn managed a half-smile. 'Thanks, Mr Saunders. I'm

OK. It throws you a sucker punch every so often. You mentioned there were still a few things to sort out?'

'Hymns,' Saunders said in a pious tone. 'You need to choose the hymns and let me know whether you want to say something at the service.'

'To be honest, Mr Saunders, speeches have never been my thing. I wouldn't know what to say.'

Saunders nodded. 'That's fine, Mr Flynn. I have to ask, but it's your choice. Whatever makes you comfortable.'

Flynn nodded in appreciation. 'As for hymns, my mother was the church goer. I'll have to take your lead on that.'

'Of course,' Saunders said with a flat smile. He pondered for a second. 'It was your lawyer who informed me you required the standard coffin and gown. We can upgrade if you want? But as you can appreciate, quality comes at a price.'

'Standard's fine,' Flynn said. 'I'll settle the bill once I've sold my mother's house.'

Greed flashed in Saunders' eyes. 'Of course, Mr Flynn, you take your time. I'd never dream of discussing payment at a time like this.' He shot Flynn the sincerest of smiles. 'Have you had any thoughts on the reception? A small buffet, perhaps? We work closely with a few establishments. I can get you a good discount.'

Flynn glanced down at the floor. 'The thing is, these past few years, my mother kept to herself. I'm not sure if she had any friends. She mentioned no one to me.' Flynn took a deep breath. 'A reception's a nice idea, but except for me, you, the vicar, and your ushers, I doubt if there'll be anyone else at the service.'

Saunders replied with a solemn smile. 'At least we'll lay her to rest alongside her husband. I imagine she'd find great comfort in that.'

Flynn failed to understand why. His old man had tormented his mother during her lifetime. Why let him do it for an eternity.

~

FLYNN SAT on the end of his mother's bed and stared into the open wardrobe. He'd taken most of her clothes to the charity shop. All that remained were a few blouses, an old shoe box full of photographs, and a half-drunken bottle of whisky. For medicinal purposes, she always insisted. *Helps me drop off at night. I like a drop in my tea.*

Flynn knelt on the carpet, reached into the wardrobe, and picked up the bottle of whisky. He unscrewed the cap, closing his eyes as he held the bottle to his lips. Saliva flooded the inside of his mouth as that sweet, malty smell triggered a slew of bad memories. Flynn stood, marched into the bathroom, and poured the whisky down the sink. Booze turned men into fools, and now, keeping a clear head was paramount, especially after letting his mother down when she needed him most.

Only a weak man allowed himself to slip back into the drink, and only a lowlife disrespected his mother's memory. Haines was such a man, and the thought of confronting him, Nia too, plagued Flynn's days like a persistent dull ache.

Finding them seemed a hopeless task. All he could do was ask around. Someone was bound to know something, and loyalties can turn so swiftly for the right price.

2

Eddie Roscoe had been getting up early since he was a kid. These days, in his sixty-fifth year, he felt the brunt of it. He had remained awake most of the night, continually looking at his phone, fretting about his son. Trevor hadn't called for over a day now. This meant nothing to most people. But the lad was a creature of habit. Twenty-four hours without chatting with his dad was a long time for him.

Even if Eddie wanted to stay in bed, his West Highland Terrier, Jip, barking since 5.30 am, was having none of it. Most days, Eddie walked him twice around the block. But his heart wasn't in it today, so Jip had to settle for a quick rummage through the back garden. Jip didn't allow the change in routine to pass unnoticed and scanned his food bowl with a moody eye, growling before he got stuck in.

Eddie watched him with a wistful smile. 'You'll have to make that last you for a while, mate. You're eating me out of house and home.'

Jip glanced up from his bowl.

'Don't look at me like that.' Eddie said. 'I'm not in the

mood to go anywhere today. But thanks to you, I've got to go to the shops.' Eddie shook his head and glanced up at his late wife's photograph. 'I know he can't answer me, Rosa, love. But it's better than talking to myself.'

Eddie turned the kettle on, staring through the kitchen window while he waited for it to boil. The back garden was less work in the autumn months, and with winter on the way, there would be less to do. Eddie once prided himself on his garden. No matter the season, he spent hours there and maintained it long after Rosa's death. But when Trevor left home, he lost interest, the dandelions and the poison ivy, like the loneliness inside, getting the better of him.

Trevor loved the garden when he was a kid, his private oasis, somewhere to hide when the teasing proved too much. Rosa often told the boy to take no notice. 'You're different, that's all,' she'd say. 'A bit slow, love, yes. But few can draw as good as you. Just ignore them, Trev. They'll soon tire of it.'

Eddie wished for that to be true more than anyone. But in these streets and avenues, names, like reputations, tended to stick.

Eddie sighed, turning his back on the garden as the kettle clicked. He made himself a quick brew. 'Not-so-clever-Trevor,' he said through a sigh, then took out his phone and redialed his son's number. Hearing Trevor's voicemail greeting was like listening to a ghost. Eddie had rung it countless times, yet the sound of Trevor's voice never failed to move him.

'Hiya, Trev,' Eddie said. 'It's Dad, again. Give us a call, please, mate. I'm worried sick about you. Take care, lad.' He hesitated for a second. 'Give me a call, Trev. Please, mate. Little Jip's worried too.'

Eddie trudged over to the kitchen table and slumped

into a chair. He dialled the number of the B&B where Trevor had been staying, letting it ring until someone answered.

'Knightleigh Hotel,' said an aggrieved sounding voice.

'Mr Boyle?'

'Speaking. How can I help you?'

'It's Eddie. Eddie Roscoe. Trevor's dad. I wondered if you had any updates or if you've remembered anything you might have missed?'

Boyle answered with a histrionic sigh. 'No, Mr Roscoe. Nothing has come to mind. Your son checked out the other day. He seemed happy enough to me. That's all I can tell you. Nothing's changed since you called me eight hours ago.'

Eddie hated being a pest. 'If anything comes to mind–'

'You'll be the first to know,' Boyle said, then hung up before Eddie could reply.

∼

EDDIE USUALLY SHOPPED AWAY from the city, although when the weather was good, he and Jip sat in the gardens of the Cathedral. The outskirts suited him most, the local shops and pubs, and, if he had a mind to, the eateries out on the fringes. He'd been going there for years; dingy by modern standards, those dimly lit bars and greasy spoon cafes were the places where he felt most comfortable. And with Rosa never allowing him to fence stolen goods at home, they served as his place of business.

Eddie sold information, too. Never to the police, of course. Grassing wasn't his style. But over the years, he'd befriended so many people; and with a face and demeanour as approachable as Eddie's, folk tended to open up to him. Eddie never understood why. 'It's because you've got a kind face and a good heart,' Rosa often told him. 'People can see that.'

'I look daft, you mean,' Eddie would joke. 'My round nose and bald head make me look like a garden gnome.'

Such comments always made Rosa laugh, and Eddie managed a weak smile as he stared into his mug of tea.

The café where he sat today was called the Ritz. Eddie had no idea who originally named the place. But looking at the white Formica tables, the plastic chairs, the slippery vinyl floor, and wood-panelled walls, they certainly had a good sense of humour. A guy called Marco owned it now. Italian, if his accent was anything to go by. A no-nonsense kind of bloke who kept his prices fair and made an excellent egg and bacon sarnie.

Eddie only popped in for a quick brew. He needed to rest his legs. Jip's dog food seemed to grow heavier with each trip. The café was quiet at this time of day. Not that Eddie minded. He needed time to think. And with Trevor's whereabouts consuming his every thought, he welcomed the lack of distraction.

Trevor lived by his routine. The lad was lost without them. He phoned Eddie every day, twice if he was fed up. Not calling was so unlike him. Messaging certainly wasn't Trevor's thing. The boy could barely read or write. Eddie tried calling him again, slamming the phone down in frustration when it failed to get a reception.

'Hey,' Marco said from behind the counter. 'What's wrong, my friend? You look upset. This isn't like you.'

'Sorry,' Eddie said. 'I've just got a few things on my mind, that's all.' He gestured to stand. 'Jip'll be fretting. I best be off.'

'Have a sandwich first. On the house. You'll feel better with some food inside you.'

Eddie couldn't disagree. He'd hardly eaten for days and sank back into his chair. 'Thanks, Marco. But I'll pay you. Don't look like that. I want nothing for free.'

Marco answered with a smile, then cracked open an egg into the frying pan. As Eddie watched it crackle and spit, he felt a cold draft as the café door opened. Brian Shelton showed his gloomy face, the potent smell of cigarettes following him. He drew back a chair and sat down, slapping his nicotine-stained hands down on Eddie's table.

'Where've you been, Eddie? I've been asking after you for days now?'

Eddie shot him a vexed look. Most people found Brian hard work. Usually, Eddie put up with him. But with Trevor on his mind, Brian's rugged, weasel-like face was unbearable. 'Well, you've found me now, haven't you? What's so urgent?'

'Mr Potato Head.'

Eddie rubbed the tiredness from his eyes. 'You should keep off the drink, Brian. What the hell are you going on about?'

'The Mr Potato Head toy from that kid's film. It's my granddaughter's birthday next week. I foolishly promised her one. Now she won't stop harking on about it.'

Eddied nodded. 'What do you expect me to do?'

'Wondered if you could get me one on the cheap. Even online, they cost a fortune.'

Eddie nodded. 'Leave it with me.'

Brian beamed. 'Cheers, Eddie. You're a star. And if I hear of anyone asking for owt, I'll make certain to pass it your way.'

3

Flynn's mother had been buried three days when he got the call. It was a nervous sounding voice, stuttering and hoarse, and Flynn interrupted the man, who used the name Brian, twice to ask if he was legit.

'Of course,' Brian assured him. 'Have no fear of that, Mr Flynn. I'd never mess people around with something as important as this, especially a man with your reputation.'

Flynn's dislike for Brian increased the longer he spoke with him. 'And what reputation might that be?'

'Nothing but good,' Brian was quick to reply. 'Jack Meadows mentioned you'd done time together in Walton.'

Flynn didn't answer and, after a long pause, said, 'Spit it out, man. What is it you have to tell me?'

'Not me. I'm more of a broker, so to speak. I introduce folk to those who know.'

Flynn sighed. 'You sound like a time waster to me. I've spread the word around. If your friend's in the know, then surely he can call me himself.'

Brian gulped. 'He's kind of retired. He doesn't get out much.'

Flynn laughed. 'That's not a smart career move for an informant.'

'It wasn't supposed to sound like that. What I meant to say was he no longer advertises. Folk tend to find him.'

'Tell me where he is then.'

Brian's voice became hoarser. 'That's why I'm calling. I'm happy to pass on your requirements and pass on his details to you in return. All we need to do is to agree on a finder's fee.'

Flynn shook his head at the phone. 'Sounds like you want money for nothing. What if your friend doesn't have anything?'

'I'd never dream of asking for any money up front, Mr Flynn. No good info, then no fee.'

'Fine,' Flynn said, 'text me the details,' then got off the phone before this self-serving leech could reply.

4
———

Of all the things people accused Brian Shelton of, Eddie agreed with two: He was a money grabber and a blabbermouth. Eddie never paid attention to a man's shortcomings unless that man placed him in an awkward situation. Brian had only ripped him off once, but that was a long time ago, and he had since made amends, and Eddie wasn't one to bear a grudge.

But Eddie's patience was wearing thin, especially with Brian's annoying habit of setting up meetings before Eddie got wind of any information. Eddie could easily have said no. But old habits die hard, and curiosity got the better of him. He'd dug deep to find out what Flynn needed to know, called in all his favours for this one.

Experience had taught him that men like Ned Flynn paid decent money for the correct information. Such transactions never came without risk. That's why he demanded they meet in the Raven. If things turned ugly, Eddie wanted a few friendly faces around him.

Admittedly, he needed the cash. But with Trevor going AWOL, he had bigger things to worry about. He'd considered telling the police, registering Trevor as a missing person. Eddie didn't entertain the idea for too long, knowing there was little they could do except ask him to fill in a form. Even if they had a lead, he doubted they would try. Sadly, people like Trevor were thought of as disposable.

Eddie took a swig of lager from his half-pint glass. He'd never been one for drinking, grimacing at the bitter taste in his mouth. He tapped his fingers on the table, releasing a deep sigh as he glanced at his watch. Poor timing was one of his pet hates. 1 pm sharp, they agreed, and it had already gone twenty-five past. 'Hurry up, for God's sake,' Eddie said beneath his breath, regretting the words the moment they left his mouth.

The broad man walking towards him stood well over six feet. His short-cropped hair bore flecks of grey, and his chiselled jaw line was covered with five o'clock shadow. Eddie had him down as early to mid-thirties. Yet the world-weary look in his eyes belonged to someone much older.

'Eddie?' the man said with a frown.

Eddie flashed him a smile. 'That's right. I take it you're Ned Flynn.' Eddie motioned to get up. 'What are you drinking?'

'Nothing,' Flynn said. 'I've given the stuff up.'

Eddie rested his arms on the table, watching attentively while Flynn pulled back a chair and sat opposite. 'So,' Flynn said. 'What do you have for me?'

Eddie tried playing it cool. 'What do you want to know?' he said, clenching his muscles as he tried to stop himself from shaking.

Flynn studied him for a moment. 'I'm looking for some friends of mine. A woman called Nia Mason and her boyfriend, Martin Haines.'

Eddie sipped his lager. 'What do you want them for?'

'That's none of your business.'

Eddie gave him his friendliest smile. 'In a way, it is, Mr Flynn. Sure, you're paying me for information. But I need to know about your intentions. I'm too old for repercussions. A man my age can't afford to be constantly looking over his shoulder.'

Flynn shook his head, smiled. 'You've nothing to worry about. They're just old friends. I miss their company. I'm desperate to get reacquainted.'

Eddie chuckled. 'You don't strike me as a man afflicted by loneliness.'

Flynn didn't answer, but Eddie was wise enough not to question his motives again.

In the brief silence that followed, Eddie studied the scars on Flynn's hands. Hardly any marred his face. That didn't surprise Eddie. Ned Flynn was a one-off, a natural fighter with great instincts. He imagined Flynn's opponents never even landed a punch.

Flynn looked over his shoulder, then fixed Eddie with a stare. 'Spit it out then.'

Eddie glanced down at the table. 'It doesn't work like that, Mr Flynn. I can't just give you what I know for free. We need to establish what it's worth. Negotiate a fair price.'

Flynn stared into Eddie's eyes. The scariest look he'd seen in ages. 'I could always just drag you outside and beat it out of you.'

Eddie took a deep swig of lager. 'You could. And I've no doubt you're skilled at doing that. But you don't strike me as a fool. Word gets around about stuff like that. I know too many people. In the long run, it wouldn't be good for you.'

'Be even worse for you.'

Eddie gripped his glass and took a deep breath. 'I'm

getting old. It wouldn't take a lot to hurt me. But I still wouldn't tell you anything.'

Flynn leaned back in his chair. 'Fair enough. But after all this palaver, I'm not convinced you've got anything to say.'

Eddie nodded, then slowly pushed his drink away from him. 'I heard you did a job for John Mason.'

Flynn shrugged. 'Anyone with their ear to the ground would have gotten wind of that.'

'Would they know that you went to fetch his wife? That she ran off with a preacher of some sort. It's odd that you're looking for Martin Haines. They reported him drowned last I heard. Perhaps it's a clairvoyant you need if you're hunting ghosts?'

Flynn sat up. 'Very impressive. How did you come to know this?'

'A good friend told me; he's an acquaintance of *Hugh Cresswell*.'

'Cresswell,' Flynn said through gritted teeth.

Eddie smiled. 'Thought that would get a response. Now is that enough to convince you?'

'When was the last time you spoke to this friend of yours?'

'That's for me to know and for you to find out.'

'How much?'

Eddie shook his head. 'I've got everything I need. On this occasion, money's the wrong question.'

Flynn clenched his fist, and, for a moment, it looked as though he was about to smash it down on the table. 'Stop playing games. What then?'

'I want you to help me with something. Think of it as an exchange of services.'

Flynn rubbed his forehead and sighed. 'What services?'

'I want you to help me find someone.'

Flynn shot him an incredulous look. 'Isn't that why I've come to you?'

'Yes,' Eddie said. 'But my boy's gone missing. And I need you to help me find him.'

'From what you told me just now, it seems you already know lots of dangerous people who can help with that.'

Eddied smiled. 'OK, I exaggerated, but I used to, a long time ago.'

Flynn shook his head. 'Nah, sorry, no can do. Money, yes, but not my time. I've got enough of my own troubles to worry about.'

'Well, that's the only way you'll get any info from me. It's your call, Mr Flynn. Take it or leave it.'

5

During the drive home, Flynn kept thinking about Eddie Roscoe's offer. The old man had some nerve, and the last thing Flynn wanted was to be traipsing off to another part of the country. Besides, he needed to focus on his own troubles, and although finding missing people lay well within his skill set, it was what led him into all this mess in the first place. No, people were only out for themselves. That undertaker, and Eddie's friend Brian, were testimony to that. Flynn had learned the hard way, and he'd had his fill of playing the saint of lost causes.

The best thing he could do was to sit tight. Something was bound to turn up. Old Eddie had already told him too much. All Flynn had to do was keep getting the message out. Someone would fill in the gaps, eventually. Greed would ensure that, but the question that kept rearing its grisly head was for how much? Flynn wasn't entirely destitute, but until he sold his mother's house, he was in no position to offer any pay-outs

The estate agent urged him to hold out for the best price, but Flynn remained unconvinced. Houses didn't sell quickly in this area. His mother's place was too near the road and, to make matters worse, a stone's throw from the notorious Moor Estate. To add to that, the house was in a state of ill repair. Damp blighted the bedroom walls, and those old windows had been letting in the cold for years now.

Flynn wandered through the vacant rooms. It broke his heart to see his mother's place so deserted, a lifetime of scrimping and saving just for this. A curtain flapped against an open window, reminding him of his time at Nia's cottage, which, although only weeks ago, felt like years now.

In his mind's eye, he pictured Nia on the sands and Haines' ghostly figure, watching them from a distance. Haines was more man than spirit. Flynn was sure of it. A chancer who faked his own death and played Flynn for a fool all the way.

Flynn clenched his jaw, balled his icy hands into fists. He didn't have time to sit it out. Every wasted minute made him more impatient. Eddie Roscoe was his best and only chance. Who was he trying to kid?

6

Eddie had just returned from walking Jip when he saw the four missed calls on his phone. He'd tried calling Trevor last night and most of the morning, and hoping the calls were from his son, felt a pang of disappointment as he recognised Flynn's number.

Slumping into his chair with a sigh, Eddie shoved the phone away from him. He tried distracting himself by reading the newspaper but only managed to flick through a few pages. He'd no time for other people's troubles today, and as though sensing his master's distress, Jip trotted towards him and rested his head on Eddie's lap.

Eddie stroked Jip's head. 'I don't know anyone else who could help us. All I know is thieves and rouges, but they'd be no use to us, mate. We need someone like Ned Flynn. Hard hitters get folks talking. An old man and a little dog won't find poor Trevor on their own.'

Eddie wiped a tear from his eye. 'We need to do something, mate.' He gazed up at his wife's photograph. 'We can't desert poor Trev; otherwise, Rosa will come back and haunt us.'

Eddie grabbed his phone, skimmed through the list of missed calls before pressing the big red label that said *Voice Messages*. Even when recorded, Flynn's voice carried an edge of menace. Eddie pictured Flynn's eyes and that dark accusing look of his.

Eddie listened to each message twice before deleting them. He glanced down at Jip. 'Who's he trying to kid. "*Considered my offer.*" He's had no luck elsewhere, more like.' Eddie gave Jip a gentle pat. 'What do you reckon, mate? Call him now? Or let him sweat?'

Wishing he had a choice, Eddie dialled Flynn's number. It would have felt good to teach this bruiser a lesson, but petty delays were for lesser men and Eddie couldn't bear the thought of Trevor suffering unnecessarily. Flynn was quick to answer. 'Hello, Mr Flynn,' Eddie said. 'You seem like a man desperate for a phone call.'

Flynn answered with an irritated sigh.

Reluctant to press his luck, Eddie softened his tone. 'Only jesting, I'm glad you've *reconsidered*. Let me text you my address. Once you're here, we'll run through what's needed.'

'No pubs,' Flynn said, 'feel safer now?'

This time Eddie was the one to sigh. 'People will know you're coming. Don't think you won't be watched.'

'Never doubted it,' Flynn said sarcastically. 'Housing estates are renowned for their top security.'

Eddie suppressed a laugh. 'Be here tomorrow. On-time if you can. No later than 12.30.'

'Yes, Boss. Anything else?'

'Bring an overnight bag. I want to get moving as soon as we can.'

7

Flynn didn't sense any surveillance as he stood outside Eddie's bungalow. Perhaps the poodle being walked was a tracker dog, or Eddie's chief lookout was the old woman nosing from the opposite window. Flynn shook his head and smiled, half expecting to be ambushed by a gang of OAPs as he rang Eddie's doorbell.

Flynn couldn't decide which was more pathetic, the Westie's fierce growl or the melodramatic bark that preceded it.

Eddie let Flynn in. 'The kitchen's that way. I'll put Jip in the parlour for a bit.'

'Fine,' Flynn said, 'as long as you feel comfortable without his protection.'

'It's easy to mock what you don't understand. Jip must like you. Otherwise, he'd rip your throat out.'

Flynn shook his head in disbelief, then went and sat in the kitchen.

A few minutes later, Eddie joined him. 'Cup of tea?'

'Wouldn't mind a coffee if you're offering.'

Eddie nodded in compliance, eyeing Flynn surreptitiously as he flicked the kettle on. Neither man tried to engage in small talk, and even once the drinks were served, they sat opposite each other, sipping their hot beverage in a restrained half-silence.

'So, what's all this about?' Flynn said, eventually.

A pained look settled in Eddie's eyes. 'My son, Trevor. I think he's in trouble. It might even be worse than that. I haven't heard from him.'

Flynn nodded. 'Right. How old is he?'

'Twenty-two.'

'Old enough to look after himself then.'

'In most cases, yes. I'd agree with you.' Eddie glanced down at his mug. 'But with Trevor, it's different.'

'In what way?'

'Let's say he has a few problems.'

'Drugs, drink, you mean?'

Eddie shook his head. 'No, nothing like that. We brought Trev up too well.' He hesitated for a second. 'He's... He's what people might call slow like.'

'Simple, you mean?'

Eddie shot Flynn a furious look. 'That's never a word I'd use. True, Trevor isn't academically bright. But he's skilled with his hands.' Eddie's voice thickened. 'The lad can make anything he puts his mind to.' Eddie's eyes glistened. 'What I mean is that he's slow with people. He's naive, a kind soul. The poor lad's too trusting.'

Flynn frowned. 'If he's so vulnerable, then why did you let him go off on his own?'

Eddie folded his arms across his chest. 'I didn't let him just go off. I've always kept an eye on him. But the lad's got wanderlust, has done since he was a kid. He's always wanted to do his own thing. Me and my Rosa, God rest her soul, did our best. I've always encouraged him to be independent so he can take care of himself once I'm gone.'

Flynn remained quiet, his regret for taking on the job increasing as Eddie grew more agitated. He reached in his pocket for a cigarette, suddenly remembering he'd quit. 'If your son's that independent. What's all the worry about?'

Eddie gave Flynn a look as though it was the stupidest question he could have asked. 'He's independent with *my help*. I get him his contract jobs, sort his digs out. He won't do anything without asking me first.'

Flynn nodded. 'Where was he living?'

'A bed-and-breakfast in Sandelby.'

'Lincolnshire coast, never imagined there was much work there this time of year.'

'He's renovating the pier.'

'What did the B&B say?'

'That he checked out a few days ago.'

'And you haven't heard from him since?'

Eddie lowered his head, then wiped something from his eye. 'I've been calling and calling. I–' He fell silent for a moment, balled his hand into a fist as tears welled in his eyes. He took a deep breath. 'I'm at my wit's end. We need to find him. I know what you're going to say. But me and the police don't mix. I don't want them sniffing around here. Even if I was a model citizen, they wouldn't achieve anything.'

Flynn held out his hands. 'Relax, Eddie. If you've done your homework, then you'd know I'd never say that. Police are the last thing I need. We'll trace your lad's steps. Ask around. I understand you're upset. But I've also suffered a recent loss. Trust me, from experience, the worst thing you can do is let your emotions get the better of you.'

Eddie nodded. 'You're right. I'm old enough to know

better. I heard about your mother, and I'm sorry for your loss. No one ever truly gets over that.' Eddie held his mug to his mouth and gulped down the rest of his tea. 'Do you think we'll find him?'

Flynn shrugged. 'It's hard to say. But we'll definitely retrace his steps.'

Eddie smiled. 'What makes you so sure?'

'I used to do this for a living, remember.'

8

They drove to Sandelby in Eddie's old camper van. Flynn's idea. It was less fuss than hiring a car, less costly too, especially if they needed to stay a few nights. Eddie accused Flynn of being cheap. Not that Flynn cared. Folk called him worse names than that. The journey started well. Both men remained quiet, Flynn focusing on the road while Eddie tended to Jip. Occasionally, Flynn caught Eddie's glances and managed to ignore them for a good while during their journey.

They had just passed Richendale when Eddie said, 'I had you down as the quiet type, but are we going to spend the entire trip in silence?'

'We've said all we need to. What else is there to say?'

Eddie shook his head. 'Didn't your parents ever teach you the value of a good conversation?'

Flynn shot him a warning look. 'My old man never taught me squat, and as for my mother, she told me not to talk to strangers.'

Eddie smiled. 'Wise words, but from what I can see, you

don't seem like a man who had the good sense to follow her advice.'

Flynn didn't answer, sighing as Eddie said, 'I asked around about you.'

'Did you, now? No doubt folk swamped you with good references.'

Eddie laughed. 'Not really. Few had a kind word to say. Most told me to stay clear of you.'

Flynn nodded. 'You should have taken notice.'

'I would have in normal circumstances.' Eddie slipped his hand in his pocket, drew out a small dog treat and fed it to Jip. 'No regrets then?'

Flynn shrugged. 'What's done is done. That's all behind me.'

'Finally learning something, huh?'

Flynn frowned. 'A lifetime of being a mug takes its toll. I've had my fill of being a slow learner.'

Flynn cast Eddie a glance, feeling the old man's eyes bore into him.

'This Nia woman,' Eddie said. 'What are you going to do when you find her?'

'That's for me to know. It's not your concern. You've got your son to think about.'

~

AT THE THOUGHT OF TREVOR, Eddie became more pensive, withdrawing further into himself until absorbed in silence. He sought distraction by gazing through the window. The faces in every passing car triggered so many memories, as did the distant fields, the houses, and the factories beyond them. He took out his mobile and called Trevor's number. *"This person's phone is currently unavailable,"* said the woman's voice, and as pleasant as it was, her words stressed the emptiness inside him.

He stroked Jip's head, revelling in the Westie's warm body pressed against his skin.

'First port of call is the B&B,' Eddie said, his eyes locked on the road.

Flynn didn't answer, but Eddie continued, nevertheless. 'Let me do the talking. Folks tend to warm to me. All you'll do is scare them off.' He ignored the aggrieved look on Flynn's face. 'The more I think about it, it's probably best you wait in the van. Just show your face when it's needed.'

'You make it sound like I'm a freak. I do this for a living, remember.'

Eddie shot him one of his disapproving looks. 'Going by your latest antics, you haven't done a very good job of it.'

Although tempted to say more, the wisdom of his years held Eddie silent. Rumours concerning Flynn's antics had come to him in droves. One implied that Flynn might have been responsible for John Mason's death. Eddie kept an open mind. Anything was possible, but there was little doubt that Flynn was dangerous. He closed his eyes to that thought, letting the flow of traffic wash over him.

∽

IF THE OLD man wasn't asleep, he did a great job faking it. Flynn shook his head; he'd never heard such loud snoring. The little Westie was sleeping too, its eyes shut tight, the tongue lolling slightly as though seeking to imitate its master. Eddie seemed like a decent enough bloke. But all his efforts to lead a regular life had led him to this: alone and broken-hearted. These days, Flynn needed no convincing that life was better lived alone. *Looking after number one* remained an easy mantra. Not that Eddie would ever feel that. His love and devotion for his son doomed him to be forever broken-hearted.

Flynn had seen jobs like this before. Mostly it was people who wanted to remain lost. Or those that didn't seldomly surfaced. From what Eddie had told him, the prospect of finding Trevor didn't sound good. The lad was too reliant on his father, and the boy's sudden disappearance had tragedy written all over it. For Flynn, it was a tale all too familiar. To his credit, Eddie appeared more philosophical than most, and no doubt, the old man had seen more than his share of darkness. A flicker of hope still lingered in Eddie's eyes. Flynn knew how he felt. He'd held such optimism once–a deluded notion. The misguided belief that things would get better and misfortune only happened to someone else.

~

A HINT of fantasy drifted through Eddie's dream, but the illusion remained strong enough to draw him in. He basked in the warm sunspots of a familiar summer. Children's laughter rang in the distance while Rosa pottered about in the garden. Jip, his little body outstretched, dozed at his master's feet. A cloudless blue sky showed little sign of easing, and the midday sun shone fiercely, baking the earth and everything that dared to idle beneath it for too long.

Eddie, from the comfort of an old deck chair, watched young Trevor kick his football across the lawn. Trevor must have been eight or nine years old. The best times in Eddie's mind. A cool beer eased the dryness in Eddie's throat while the smell of hot dogs and fried onions mingled with the sea air. Eddie focused on his son's smile, a sudden sense of loss urging him to beckon the boy closer. Trevor ran towards him, but the lad's efforts proved fruitless because no matter how hard he tried to reach his father, the same distance stood between them. Eddie rose from his chair and shouted Trevor's name, his desperation intensifying as his voice grew louder.

'Help me, Dad,' Trevor cried. *'Help me.'*

But Eddie could not move, his legs like leaden weights as fear overwhelmed him.

Eddie woke with a sudden jolt, startling Jip so much that the little Westie spent the next few minutes growling.

He shot Flynn a furious glance. 'What are you gawping at?'

'You,' Flynn said. 'One minute you're snoring your head off, the next you're shouting.'

Eddie stroked Jip to calm him, and looking at Flynn, he said, 'Isn't a man allowed to dream?'

'*Dream*,' Flynn scoffed. 'You sounded more like a man caught in a nightmare.'

Eddie glared at him. 'Aye, and you'd know all about *that*.'

9

Sandelby remained pretty much as Eddie remembered. In the central part of town, the grand clock tower, seated on the island roundabout, looked worse for wear. Its red-bricked body appeared weathered and cracked, and the lead weathervane atop of its slate spire had a slight bent to it. Yet for all its ailments, it still looked magnanimous compared to the tired-looking shops, the littered pavements and neglected funfair, and those desolate wet sands where world-weary donkeys stared aimlessly out to sea.

The Knightleigh Hotel impressed Eddie even less. From the outside, it appeared to be nothing more than a typical four-bedroom house. Eddie tapped Flynn's arm. 'You just stand there and look mean. Let me do all the talking.'

As they stepped into the hallway, the makeshift pine reception area gave little suggestion that it was a four-star B&B. The proprietor, Ian Boyle, was equally banal. Tall and pot-bellied, his thinning, greasy hair fell lankly across his forehead. His white cotton shirt bore a tidemark on the collar, and there was an olive tinge to his black polyester slacks. Boyle's voice complimented his appearance; it was deep and hoarse the voice of a man who had surrendered all hope of ever quitting the cigarettes.

Boyle flashed them a nicotine-stained smile. 'Yes, Gents, how can I help you? Pre-booking or are you after a vacancy?'

Eddie looked Boyle in the eye. 'I'm here about my son, Trevor Roscoe. I spoke with you yesterday morning.'

Boyle frowned. 'Hmm, Mr Roscoe,' he said through a sigh. 'Nothing's changed since I last spoke with you, I'm afraid.'

'I was hoping you might have remembered–'

'Nope,' interrupted Boyle. 'I've told you everything I know.'

'So, you keep telling me,' Eddie said. 'I'm here to ask around, all the same, retrace his steps. Perhaps if I'm able to do that, it might even jog your memory.'

'I wish you the best of luck with that, Mr Roscoe.'

'The name's Eddie. The thing is, Mr Boyle.'

'Ian, please.'

'The thing is, Ian, even the best of us forget sometimes.'

Boyle answered with a stiff smile. 'I've been racking my brains since the first time we spoke. Nothing's come to me. I get the impression you think I'm lying about something.'

'*Lying?*' Eddie said. 'That's an odd thing to say. What makes you think that?'

Boyle rubbed the back of his neck. 'You're very persistent.'

'I'm just trying to find my son, that's all.'

'I get that, Eddie, but I've told you all I know.'

Eddie stretched his arms, then rolled his neck in a half-circle. 'Been in that van for hours. When you get to my age, the last thing the body needs is more stiffness.' He regarded Boyle for a moment. 'So, Trevor didn't bother with anyone?'

Boyle shook his head. 'Not as far as I know. The lad would get up early, have his brecky, then, until he came back from work around six in the evening, that's all I'd see of him.'

'Where would he go for his tea?'

'Chippy mostly, sometimes the wife would make him something.'

Eddie smiled. 'That's very kind of you. Trevor never told me that.' He hesitated for a minute, leaning his head to one side. 'What about work colleagues?'

Boyle shrugged. 'Can't help you there. All I know is what I've told you. No one ever came here. As far as I could tell, your boy kept himself to himself.'

'And you can't recall anything else?'

'No,' Boyle said. 'I'm truly sorry. If anything comes to mind, I mean anything, trust me, Eddie, you'll be the first to know.'

Eddie pressed his lips into a thin line. 'Call me on my mobile if anything comes to mind. I'm here for a few days, so I'll be straight over.'

Boyle touched his throat. 'Where are you staying, if you don't mind me asking?'

'My camper van.'

'I hope it's comfy.'

'It does me.'

Boyle nodded. 'I've vacancies should you change your mind. I can do you a good price.'

'I'll bear that in mind,' Eddie said with a forced smile. 'And thanks again for your cooperation.'

10

As they walked back to the van, Flynn never spoke a word. He could sense Eddie's eyes prompting him to speak, and it wasn't until they were inside that Eddie said, 'Come on then, out with it?'

Flynn frowned. 'What makes you think I've got anything to say?'

'You've got that look on your face. I've wasted enough time with you to know when you're thinking.'

'Am I that easy to read?'

'Yes and no,' Eddie said. 'I've spent a lifetime studying people's faces. You'd be amazed by what they tell you.'

'So, you know Boyle's lying then?'

'Of course, I do. He couldn't even look me in the eye.'

Flynn nodded. 'I'm glad you spotted that.'

'Noticing things is easy enough. The trouble is, what are we going to do about it?'

'Did you smell the beer on him?'

Eddie nodded. 'Yeah, and his BO. What's that got to do with anything?'

'Seems like Boyle likes his drink. He doesn't strike me as

a man willing to travel too far. Let's find someplace to park this heap, and we'll check out some nearby pubs, see what folk have to say about him.'

∼

FLYNN FOUND a spot in one of the quieter car parks, which, much to Eddie's disapproval, charged £4.50 for the entire day. Flynn felt the price was fair, unlike Eddie, who griped on about it like a man recently robbed of his life savings. He kept complaining all the way to the Six Bells pub, a dimly lit dive within walking distance from the Knightleigh Hotel.

For Flynn, pubs like the Six Bells were all too familiar. With their shoulders stooped, a line of regular drinkers stood along the bar. Most were middle-aged men, with the old boys preferring the corner tables. A group of youths played pool, and a lone woman dressed younger than her years sipped her wine silently from the exalted position of a bar stool. She watched Flynn's every move, her heavily made-up eyes unwavering as they pursued him to the bar.

'Seems like you have an admirer,' Eddie said.

Flynn didn't answer. Instead, he lifted his hand, keeping it raised until he attracted the barman's attention.

'Yes, Gents?'

Flynn assumed the barman was over eighteen, although the young man's appearance suggested he was still in high school. His fresh-looking skin was a marked contrast to the beer-weathered faces that surrounded him. His voice was lighter too. His black short-sleeved shirt and matching trousers were clean and neatly pressed. It was as though he'd wandered in the bar by mistake and had been stuck here ever since.

Flynn ordered himself a Coke and Eddie asked for a

bitter shandy. Flynn shook his head in disbelief; he'd never imagined himself ordering a soft drink in a dive like this. Only weeks ago, he'd been high on whisky, Nia reeling him in like a love-struck fool, while Haines got into his head convincing him he was haunted by his ghost. Flynn grimaced, the thought of such treachery settling like a vile taste in the mouth. He held the expression for a few seconds until the man standing to his right said, 'Cheer up, mate. It might never happen.'

Flynn turned around, watching the confident smirk on the man's face disappear as Flynn stared into his sleepy, bloodshot eyes. 'How do you know it hasn't already happened?' Flynn said.

The man's face and neck turned a rich shade of crimson. 'I don't. I was just saying that's all, joking, trying to make polite talk.'

Aware of the sudden silence, Flynn sensed Eddie staring at him. He needed to turn the conversation around, or Eddie would never let him hear the last of it. 'I know you were,' Flynn said. 'It's been a long day, that's all.'

The man's shoulders sagged. 'Let me get you another.'

'Wouldn't dream of it,' Flynn said. 'This one's on me. What are you having?'

'Whisky and water would be nice.'

'Double?'

'That's very kind of you.' The man studied Flynn for a second, the fear in his eyes diminishing. He held out his hand. 'The name's Jack.'

Flynn shook his hand. 'Ned.' He nodded at Eddie. 'This is Eddie, my father-in-law.'

Thankfully, Eddie remained stony-faced. He flashed Jack a smile then sipped his pint, allowing Flynn to do the talking.

Jack emptied his glass with one big gulp. He stood quietly for a moment, beads of sweat glistening on his bald head. 'Haven't seen you fellas in here before. What on earth brings you to this place?'

'We're having a holiday drive along the coast, stopping at different towns. Thought we'd look at Sandelby.'

Dolly make-up laughed from her bar stool. 'God knows why,' she said. 'This is a scab of a town. A place where northerners come to die.'

Jack scowled at her. 'Be quiet, Alice. No one asked you to chirp in.' He turned to Flynn and raised his eyes. 'She's been drinking since early morning; she does have a point, though.'

Flynn nodded. 'Perhaps, but we're only passing through.'

Jack glanced down at his glass. 'There are better places than the Six Bells.'

'Sure,' Flynn said. 'We'll venture into town once we've rested. At the moment, we're trying to find a decent B&B. There's a lot of choice. Eddie's tired of walking around. So, we nipped in here for a drink.'

Eddie raised his glass. 'Not a bad pint too.' He caught Jack's eye. 'How long have you lived here, Jack?'

'Since I was born.'

'You must know the town as good as anyone. What about places to stay? Got any recommendations?'

Jack shook his head. 'You're asking the wrong man. I've lived in council houses all my life. Never needed a B&B.'

Alice slammed her empty glass onto the bar. 'I know a few.'

'Great,' Flynn said before Eddie had time to answer. He walked over to where Alice was sitting and pointed at her glass. 'What are you drinking?'

'A dry white,' she said with a half-smile.

Flynn handed her glass to the barman. 'Make it a large one.'

Alice looked scarier at close range, and the tan foundation smeared over her face stressed the crevices and lines instead of masking them. Her hair, a thinning bouffant of auburn and grey, shone translucently against the afternoon sunlight. She stank of perfume and smoke, her world-weary eyes scrutinizing him from an outline of green shadow. 'So, where have you tried?'

'A few places around here. The best we've seen so far is the Knightleigh Hotel.'

Alice sipped her wine. 'Ian Boyle's place. It's clean enough, I suppose, as long as you sleep with your socks on.' She giggled at her own joke. 'He drinks in here a lot. I'll point him out to you if he comes in. Buy him a few ales, and he might even give you a discount.'

'I'll bear that in mind,' Flynn said with a smile. 'I take it he likes his drink?'

'Don't we all. He's harmless enough on his own, although he's a different person when he's boozing with those Pikey mates of his from Kinsale Hollow.'

Before Flynn could ask who she was referring to, Jack interrupted. 'I've told you before about using that word; there's a lot of decent people on those traveller sites, and don't run Ian down behind his back. The lad's all right; he hasn't bothered with the Finnegans in ages.'

'He bloody well has,' Alice protested. 'He's always bragging about his dodgy deals; he was drinking with Shaun and Paddy Finnegan the other day. They've been very pally ever since Boyle got a job for that soft-lad who was staying with him.'

Eddie and Flynn exchanged glances. 'Soft-lad?' Flynn said. 'I haven't heard that expression before.'

Alice rolled her eyes. 'It means thick, stupid, someone who's a bit slow.'

Flynn nodded. 'And you say this Ian Boyle got him a job. That was kind of him.'

'Boyle *kind?*' Alice scoffed. 'Don't make me laugh. He doubtless made a few quid out of it, knowing him. Those Finnegans are always looking for cheap–'

'That's enough, Alice,' interrupted Jack. 'You don't know that.'

Alice took a deep sip of wine. 'Don't tell me what I don't know.'

'Suit yourself,' Jack said. 'But you'll only bring trouble to yourself. Let's see how gobby you are once the Finnegan's get wind of it.'

Alice didn't respond. Instead, with an unsettled look on her face, she sipped her wine in silence. Once again, Flynn and Eddie shared a glance, then Flynn said, 'These Finnegans sound like a rough bunch.'

Jack shook his head and sighed. 'Trust me; you don't want to know.'

11

Eddie wasn't a violent man. Yet, with scum like Boyle, all he could think about was what he'd do once he got his hands on him. For once, Flynn had talked sense, and it seemed ironic that a man with such a brutal reputation managed to calm him. Although Eddie was happy for Flynn to take control, as he stood behind Flynn in the Hotel's hallway, he grew anxious. He questioned whether the love for his son overrode his better judgement, leading him beyond his depth, forcing him to ignore that sense of impending danger and the repercussions to come.

Initially, Boyle looked surprised. Then his face paled, a frightened look in his eyes as Flynn gripped him by the shoulders. Flynn guided him into the lounge and shoved him onto the leather sofa. Boyle tried to say something, becoming silent the instant Flynn slapped him.

Eddie looked on in awe. He sensed Flynn could have hit Boyle harder, but this was just a taster, enough to get the scruffy man's attention.

'Speak when you're spoken to,' Flynn said.

Boyle never said a word, and with Flynn's voice as convincing as it was, even Eddie felt obliged to remain silent. Flynn pushed an armchair towards Boyle and sat down in front of him. 'Why did you lie to us?'

'I never–'

Flynn slapped him again, the sound of flesh against flesh resonating so loudly that it almost made Eddie's eyes water. A door closed upstairs. 'Who's that?' Flynn said.

'Don't know,' said a frightened Boyle, 'probably one of the guests.'

Flynn nodded at Eddie. 'Stand by the door. Make sure no one comes in.'

Eddie did as he was told, even though he'd no idea what use he would be if someone tried forcing their way in.

Flynn paused for a few seconds, then, satisfied all was quiet, said, 'OK, Boyle, I'm going to ask you again, only this time you sure as hell better have a good answer.' Flynn slapped his shovel-like hands onto his lap. 'Why did you lie?'

Boyle took a deep breath. 'I was scared, I suppose.'

'Of Paddy Finnegan?'

Boyle's eyes widened with surprise.

Flynn grinned. 'Yes, I know all about him.' Flynn straightened his shoulders, causing Boyle to flinch. 'Tell us about how you helped Trevor find a new job.'

Boyle looked up at Eddie, instantly lowering his eyes when Eddie glared at him. Boyle took a few more deep breaths. 'The lad was being laid off. He–'

'Bullshit,' Eddie said. 'He would have told me if he was. The last time I heard from him, there was at least two months' work left.'

Flynn motioned for Eddie to calm down. Eddie nodded

in submission, a quick nod of the head acknowledging that he would let Flynn do the talking.

Flynn moved closer. 'So, let's assume that's true. Poor Trevor was being laid off, worried about finding work. Surely, if it was that bad, he would go home to his dad. Why the hell confide in you?'

Even in these circumstances, Boyle struggled to look Flynn in the eye. Mostly he looked down at the floor, gazing upwards now as Flynn prompted him for an answer. Boyle wiped his arm across his forehead. 'Trevor had been struggling to pay the rent. He explained to me why he'd gotten into arrears. I–'

'Nonsense,' Eddie interrupted. 'Trevor would never miss a payment. I made sure of that every week. He–'

Flynn silenced Eddie with a look, and turning towards Boyle, said, 'And what did you say when Trevor told you that?'

'I said he could pay me when he got straight. That I'd ask around to see if I could find him something.'

Flynn frowned. 'That's very charitable of you.' He paused. 'Arrears, you say?'

Boyle nodded.

'I don't remember you saying anything about that to Eddie. Or about Trevor being laid-off.'

'It must have slipped my mind.'

'Must have,' Flynn said. 'Because you swore you told us everything.' Flynn clacked his knuckles across the bridge of Boyle's nose.

'Jesus,' Boyle yelled. 'What the hell was that for?'

'Lying,' Flynn said. 'You promised Eddie you'd told him everything you knew. Helping Trevor with a job and his rent isn't something easily forgotten. It soon came to mind when I jogged your memory.'

With a trembling hand, Boyle wiped the blood from his nose. 'He had enough on his mind. I didn't think it was right to mention it.'

As Flynn stood up, watching his tall, broad physique tower over Boyle, even Eddie felt nervous. Menace blazed in Flynn's eyes. A look that Eddie hadn't truly witnessed until now. He was tempted to call out Boyle's lies but watching Flynn at work, he felt confident that his partner would soon draw the truth from him.

Flynn stared down at Boyle. 'We both know that's bullshit. Talk to me, Boyle. This is your last chance.'

His voice thick with fear, Boyle stammered out his answer. 'Paddy Finnegan warned me not to say anything.'

Eddie lunged towards him, stopping when Flynn blocked his way. 'You heartless bastard,' Eddie said. 'Tell me where my lad is now, or I swear to God, I'll kill you myself.'

Tears filled Boyle's eyes. 'Honest Eddie, I don't have a clue. Once I fixed him up with Paddy, that was the last I saw of him.'

'Why didn't you tell me that from the start,' Eddie said. 'God knows what's happened to my boy during the time you've wasted.'

Flynn sat down and rested a hand on Boyle's shoulder. 'I'll give you a chance to make amends. We need to speak to Paddy Finnegan. Set that up, and you might redeem yourself.'

Boyle shook his head. 'The Finnegans like to keep their business matters private. They do things off the books. Paddy would kill me if he knew I'd spoken to you.'

Flynn sighed. 'Well, you're going to die either way, sooner if you don't help me. Setting up a meeting with Paddy Finnegan gives you a few extra days. Now that's what I call a bargain, don't you?'

12

Both Eddie and Flynn hadn't liked the arrangement from the start. Meeting a bunch of strangers out in the sticks made a bad situation worse. Not that they had any choice. Eddie would do anything to help his son. Vulnerability was the least of his worries, and no matter how much Flynn complained, Eddie remained willing to take his chances.

Paddy was over thirty minutes late, and even before he arrived, both Eddie and Flynn had lost patience. After much duress, he'd agreed to meet them miles from town, in a lay-by on a deserted B-road where the surrounding vast empty fields felt as ominous as the cloud-ridden sky.

Paddy Finnegan stood almost as tall as Flynn. A beer gut made him appear bigger, and the muscular frame from his youth was cushioned with middle-aged flab. Eddie struggled to place his age. Paddy's weather-beaten face looked like a man in his forties, yet behind the blue eyes shone a youthful exuberance. He talked like a machine gun, and Flynn had to ask him to repeat himself after every other sentence.

As expected, Paddy didn't come alone. Joining him in his grubby battered van was that scumbag Boyle and Paddy's son. Paddy never introduced him by name, just said he was there to watch his back. You could tell straight off he was his father's son, sharing that mongrel-like look of dirty blonde hair, three-day stubble, and unwashed skin; his faded checked-shirt hung loosely over his skinny frame, and the bottoms of his dusty, stained jeans were rolled up above his steel-toe capped boots.

The Finnegan's distinctive smell was a mix of dirt and sweat. Paddy's voice was loud; every brash word carried on an air of stale breath.

'As I just told ya,' Paddy said. 'I offered the lad some tarmacking work. He lasted a day; he said he couldn't take to it. I paid him cash in hand, and he went on his way.'

'To where?' Flynn said.

Paddy took a pipe out of his pocket and spent the next few minutes lighting it. He took a deep drag and blew a cloud of smoke towards Flynn. 'How the hell would I know?'

'I thought you would have asked him.'

Paddy shook his head. 'The lad was a dimwit. He let me down. I was glad to see the back of him.'

Eddie gave him a fierce look. 'That's my son you're talking about.'

Paddy grinned. 'Well, you should have taken better care of him. Most of my lads are grown men, but I wouldn't let them out of my sight, not in this world. We're a very close family.'

Flynn nodded. 'Too close by the looks of you.'

Paddy took the pipe from his mouth and, pointing the stem at Flynn, said, 'I hope you're not implying what I think you are. I don't take kindly to folk casting aspersions.'

Eddie swallowed hard, waiting for Flynn's response, the sudden rush of fear holding him silent.

Flynn stood his ground, meeting Paddy's stare with his own. 'You started it by disrespecting Eddie's son.'

Paddy looked at his boy. 'Did you hear that, Shaun? You've got a lot of balls, fella. I'm the nice guy here. Let's not forget I was in two minds about meeting you. I'm doing this as a favour.' He glanced at Boyle. 'You're the one who got nasty, threatening my friend here.'

Flynn gave Boyle a disdainful look. Eddie did too. Since the Finnegan's arrival, the scruffy man had grown in confidence.

'He brought it on himself,' Flynn said, 'the lying scumbag.'

'Hey,' Boyle protested, falling silent as Paddy looked at him and held out his hand.

Paddy stepped forward. 'He was just protecting a friend's business interests.'

'Is that right,' Flynn said. 'It sounds more like protecting those with something to hide if you ask me.'

Paddy's son, Shaun, moved away from the van and stood by his father's side. 'Shall I knock him out, Da?' he kept saying. 'Don't take any shit from him.'

Much to Eddie's surprise, Paddy remained watchful. Eddie didn't put it down to the wisdom of years. Paddy had a recklessness that confirmed his son was a chip off the old block. No, the man's hesitancy seemed due to Flynn. It was as though Paddy recognised something, a hint in Flynn's eyes perhaps, that filled the man with caution.

Paddy rested a hand on Shaun's shoulder. 'Take no notice, son. He's trying to get a bite out of ya. We've said everything we have to.' He patted the base of his pipe and let the remaining tobacco fall to the ground. 'Frigging time wasters. Bollocks to the pair of you.'

Eddie and Flynn shared a glance. Then Flynn said, 'You've told us nothing. We need more than that. Otherwise, you leave us with no choice but to go to the police.'

Paddy swung open the van door, then turned around. 'And I'll tell them the same thing. Not that they'll come. Men like you rarely fare well talking to the police.'

13

The Finnegan's van roared off into the distance, the smell of petrol lingering in its wake while Flynn and Eddie looked on quietly in the night's silence. The air had turned colder, the light fading as a defeated sun slunk behind the dark outline of the trees.

Eddie wiped a hand across his brow. 'Dirty lying scum. Talking about my boy like that. For a minute, I thought it was going to kick off.'

Flynn shook his head. 'Scum like that need bigger numbers. They like to hunt in packs.'

'Three seemed more than enough.'

'Nah, they wouldn't have done anything unless Paddy gave the word, and he knew I would have got to him first.'

Eddie released a long sigh. 'So, what do we do now?'

Flynn caught the anguish in Eddie's eyes. 'We'll visit that site of theirs. Let's check the A-to-Z. Kinsale Hollow can't be very far from here.'

Eddie nodded and strolled back to the van. Flynn followed, opened the van door, and slid back onto the driver's seat.

'According to the map,' Eddie said. 'Kinsale Hollow's only a few miles away.'

'Told you,' Flynn said.

Eddie set the map aside and stroked Jip. The little Westie responded with low groans of delight, its breath deepening and its eyes slowly closing. Eddie stared down at Jip. 'Trevor was always good with dogs.' His voice thickened. 'What do you think our chances are of finding him?'

Flynn shrugged. 'All we can do is hope. I don't know what's happened to your boy. But my gut tells me these Finnegans are at the root of it.' Flynn nodded at the dog. 'You best stay with him while I look around. Keep him calm. The last thing we need is him yapping.'

Eddie pressed his lips together. 'If you say so. He's normally good, to be fair. But far be it from me to ruin our chances.'

Flynn slotted the key in the ignition and started the engine. The little camper van spluttered into life. Flynn shifted into first, both men remaining silent while the van gained momentum. Flynn drove a steady fifty along the B-road, slowing down when it tapered off into the lanes. The bends were sharp and steep, and for a moment, Flynn feared he'd taken a wrong turn. When they reached the top of the hill, Flynn pulled over to get his bearings.

Eddie pointed towards the horizon. 'I reckon that's the Kinsale Hollow site there.'

Flynn frowned. 'Where?'

'Follow my finger to the right of those trees. Do you see that wall in the distance and those iron gates?'

Flynn nodded, then restarted the engine. 'I'll get as close as I can. It'll be safer to walk the rest.'

Flynn parked on a small gravelly lay-by near a cluster of trees. He opened the van door, stepped outside, then turned to face Eddie, resting his arms on top of the driver's seat. 'Do us a favour, pass me the metal pipe and crowbar from my holdall.'

Eddie did as Flynn asked. 'Is that going to be enough? I thought fellas like you carried a gun for when things got nasty.'

Flynn slipped the pipe into his jacket pocket, then, holding the crowbar, said, 'You'd be amazed how many scrapes this has gotten me out of, especially when you don't want to draw attention to yourself.'

Eddie didn't reply, a concerned look settling on his face as Flynn said, 'If I don't return in forty minutes, you need to get the hell out of here.'

'Do you want me to go to the police?'

Flynn shrugged. 'You do what you think is best, although I'd drive home if I were you.'

'That wouldn't do Trevor much good.'

Flynn saw the shine in Eddie's eyes. 'I'm just saying it as a last resort. Most likely, I'll be back in less than half an hour; I'll just have a quick look around, that's all.'

Flynn headed off down the lane, his long shadow engrossed in darkness as Eddie shut off the headlights. He strolled quietly; his every breath accentuated in the dead silence. Having reached the outer wall, he stepped back, squatting beneath the hedge opposite, then took in the site. It must have been four to five acres, a gated community of red-brick bungalows and assorted caravans. He inched along the hedgerow, quickening his pace as he passed the gold-tipped wrought-iron gates. Light flooded the driveway, forcing Flynn to hide in the shadows. A dog growled, then another, until they drowned out the thick beat of Flynn's heart with their fierce barking.

Flynn lay on his stomach and crawled along the verge,

the wet grass seeping through his trousers and the gravelly soil scraping across his skin. Snaking through the darkness reminded him of that fateful night at Mason's house. Bad luck hounded him like a curse. How many more times would he find himself in these types of situations? Before he could give the notion more thought, the sound of men shouting distracted him. Paddy Finnegan's boys, he guessed, quarrelling among themselves as they struggled to quieten the dogs.

It was ten minutes before they went back indoors, and even then, Flynn remained reluctant to move, both he and the night sky waiting with bated breath. Convinced it was safe, he got up and followed the outer wall, then veered off down the narrow walkway that ran parallel to the site and led to the woods behind.

It was difficult to see from the gloom of the trees. Yet from what Flynn could make out, a stretch of rough grassland separated the woods from the back end of the Finnegan site. Several dilapidated caravans hunched haphazardly throughout the field. Some were dimly lit, and the smoke tainted air carried a distant sound of voices. Flynn edged forward to take a closer look. A small group of men sat around a fire that blazed within an old oil drum, the warm glow of the flames lighting their sad faces. Their bony shoulders remained slumped. Defeat weighed heavily in their eyes, and a thin layer of dust covered their ashen skin. Flynn recognised the expression from his prison days. Dispirited and afraid, it was the look of men who had long since given up.

As Flynn tried to see if Trevor was among them, one man looked in his direction, forcing him to retreat to the safety of the trees. He glanced at his watch. Half an hour had passed. No doubt Eddie would be panicking. They needed to come back with extra muscle and confront this scumbag family in full daylight.

Making progress along the lane, Flynn was glad to see Eddie's camper van still parked on the lay-by. He quickened his pace, noticing, as he drew closer, Eddie wasn't there, and the passenger door was wide open. Flynn stood still, hesitant to call out Eddie's name, hoping the old fool had taken Jip for a stroll to quieten him.

Fixing his gaze beyond the van, Flynn caught sight of two figures walking towards him. Instinct told him to hold his ground, although experience led him to the safety of the van. He remained outside, leaning against the driver's door, slipping the crowbar from his pocket, and holding it behind his back.

Flynn dropped his guard slightly when he saw the two women walking towards him. The tallest looked in her late teens, whereas the other, short and busty, looked in her early to mid-forties. The younger one was pretty enough, her long strawberry blonde hair tied in a ponytail, her tight joggers and her close-fitting jacket drawing attention to her tiny waist and hips. The other was less pleasing to the eye. Her face had a lived-in, almost spiteful look, and her lank, shoulder-length hair was a blend of peroxide and gingery grey. The couple shared a harshness in the eyes, and as Flynn studied them more closely, it became easier to imagine how the girl would look when she grew older.

'Have you broken down?' said the older of the two.

Flynn shook his head. 'My dad's dog needed to relieve itself. He's taken it for a walk; he'll be back soon.'

The two women shared a glance, then the older one said, 'Is his dog a Westie?'

Flynn answered with a wary nod. 'Yeah, why?'

'We've just passed him. He was leaning against the farm

gate; he didn't look too good if you ask me. We asked if he needed help, but he kept insisting he was all right.'

Flynn placed the crowbar on the ground and stepped towards them. 'Thanks for telling me.' He pointed down the lane. 'The gate down there, you mean?'

The older woman nodded. 'Yeah, just around the corner. I'll show you if you like.'

'No, it's all right,' Flynn said, but before he could say another word, the couple had turned around and were walking ahead of him. Reluctantly, Flynn caught them up. He raised his collar against the cold and walked silently alongside them, watching the two women askance.

With the gate in his sights, Flynn noticed it was wide open. He shot the older woman a cautious look. 'This the one?'

'Yeah,' she said and started walking ahead of him. 'He was here a few minutes ago.' She pointed at something on the ground. 'The dog's lead is here, though.'

Flynn hurried over to inspect it. He didn't like this one bit and stood paralyzed with indecision debating whether to go looking for Eddie or call out to him. Flynn stared down at the lead and bent down to pick it up. The instant he saw two young men running towards him, he stood. Years of experience had taught him to react quickly. Yet there was little he could do as someone grabbed him from behind. His limbs struggled ineffectually against their weight, his senses blurring as a cloth doused in whisky and bleach covered his face.

PART II

1

Flynn's aching body was more tolerable than the throbbing pain in his head, and as he swallowed against the dryness in his throat, a vile brew of whisky, bleach, and urine flooded his senses. He opened his eyes, squinting at the sudden blast of daylight. Memories of last night returned to him in flashes. He winced at his own stupidity; how had those women fooled him so easily? Dwelling on it would do no good. As his mother always told him, hindsight was a wonderful thing.

On trying to sit up, Flynn became aware of his shackled hands. He rolled onto his stomach, pressed his palms onto the concrete floor and pushed himself to his knees. He tried to slip his wrists free, the chain tightening as he grew more frantic. Flynn took a deep breath, trying to calm himself while taking in his surroundings.

From what he could make out, they'd imprisoned him in one of the unfinished bungalows. The place was cold and damp; the floor cluttered with broken toys and old clothes, and piled against the newly plastered walls, stood a collection of kids' bikes. A loosely fitted plastic sheet sealed the glassless window. Flynn felt the cold air travel through his clothes, which, coupled with the concrete floor, made the room close to freezing. He tried once more to slacken the chain, but it made no difference.

Flynn stood, stepped forward, then stopped suddenly because the chain only gave him a four-foot leeway. He turned around and followed the chain to its source, a metal block concreted to the floor. There was no point in trying to pull it free; it would take a jackhammer to shift it. Flynn gave the chain a defeated look. He needed to find a way out and feared the worse for Eddie too. God knows what these lowlifes had planned for them.

∽

EDDIE WANTED to sit up the moment he opened his eyes, but the pain that riddled his body stopped him from doing so. He'd woken just after dawn, the birdsong a marked contrast to the musty smelling air and the gloomy half-light enveloping him.

It hadn't taken the Finnegan's too much effort to drag Eddie from the van. Eddie was more worried for Jip. The little Westie had tried putting up a fight, and it broke Eddie's heart to hear his little friend yelping.

'Jip,' Eddie said softly. 'Where are you, boy? Jip. Jip. Come here; there's a good boy.'

There was no response. Eddie swallowed back his tears. 'Poor Jip,' he said to himself, and it didn't bear thinking about what they might have done to him. No doubt they'd treated Trevor worse. Eddie held his head in his hands, his chin quivering, tears getting the better of him. He pictured his son and took a deep breath. 'Silly old fool,' he said to himself. 'There'll be plenty of time for that later. Crying will do you no good.'

It took Eddie another five minutes to sit up. A relentless pain surged through his ribs, and, battling with every gasp for air, it took him a while to catch his breath. For a moment, he wondered why they hadn't tied him up, but the question didn't linger in his mind for too long. Clearly, they believed he posed little threat. They'd gotten him into this caravan without a struggle. So, why shouldn't they? But Eddie had other ideas. He would never stop trying to take his boy home, and the only thing that could stop him was death.

∽

FLYNN WANTED to smack Paddy's son, Shaun, in the mouth the minute he caught sight of him. The lad stood grinning at the doorway, his wiry frame casting a spindly shadow. 'You're wasting your time pulling on that chain, big man.' Shaun's grin widened. 'You don't want to be pulling on anything else either. The worst thing you could do is waste your energy.'

Flynn frowned. 'And why is that?'

'You'll find out soon enough.' Shaun threw a plastic shopping bag at Flynn's feet. 'Da said I was to feed you, but you'd get bugger all if it were left to me.'

Flynn shot the bag a glance. 'Where is Paddy? Tell him I need to speak with him.'

Shaun shook his head. 'No can do. He's a busy man. A man who doesn't want to talk with you.'

'Where's Eddie then? I hope for your sake he's unharmed?'

'And if he isn't, big fella? What are you going to do about it?'

Flynn fixed him with a stare. 'You can't keep us here much longer. People will look for us.'

Shaun sneered. 'What people?'

'Bad people. People you and your da don't want to know.'

Shaun laughed. 'Let them come.' He turned to face the doorway, then, looking over his shoulder, said, 'You eat that food now, big fella. And don't be wasting too much thought about these *bad* people because nobody is coming; no one gives a damn about you.'

∽

EDDIE COULDN'T RECALL EVER BEING inside a caravan as miserable as this. They'd hacked out most of the interior. Dirty plates and pans filled the sink, and a dubiously stained mattress replaced the bunk bed come sofa. A rank smell tainted the air, a stench so overpowering Eddie could taste it. He tried breathing through his nose, each slow step towards the door followed by a wheezing sound from his chest.

It came as no surprise to find the door locked. Eddie still tried opening it, pressing as much weight into it as his tired body allowed, his trembling hand repeatedly pushing down on the handle. Such efforts proved futile. His old bones could take no more punishment, forcing him to rest on his haunches before he dropped.

It took Eddie another thirty minutes to get up. At least his breathing was steadier now, and his body felt more rested. He banged his fist against the door. 'Let me out,' he shouted. 'Let me out. Come on, you cowardly bastards.'

Eddie kept this up until he heard someone unlock the

door, falling back against the boarded window as they kicked it open.

The young man standing against a backdrop of grey light looked no more than sixteen. Eddie recognised him from last night, a skinny, pasty-faced youth with greasy shoulder-length hair. The runt of the litter, who, provoked by his older brothers, had been too free with his kicks and punches. Even now, the lad wore an air of spite. 'Keep it shut, old man,' he said through gritted teeth. 'Don't make things worse for yourself.'

'I need to pee,' Eddie said. 'You let me out of here.'

'Do it inside. There's a can in the corner.'

Eddie considered charging at him then making a run for it, but his sore bones convinced him otherwise. This was just a kid and a stupid one at that. Eddie lowered his eyes. 'What's your name, son?'

'I'm not your son.'

'No, you're definitely not. But you must have a name?'

'Ady. Aiden.' The lad paused. 'Mr Finnegan to you.'

'Where do you get off talking to people like that? I'm not a dog. I'm old enough to be your grandfather.'

A questioning look flashed in Aiden's eyes. A moment of self-reflection that was quickly erased by his idiotic smile. 'I'll talk to you how I like. Once you've rested, Da said you'll be working under me.'

Eddie felt his face burn. 'I'm not working for you, you little prick.'

Aiden glared at him. 'You will if you want to help that idiot son of yours.'

Eddie jerked his head back. 'What the hell have you done to him?'

'Fed him and given him a home.' Aiden stuck his chest

out. 'He does as he's told. Unlike some, he knows what's good for him.'

Eddie edged forward, causing Aiden to step back. The lad glanced to his left, and, as though Eddie was a savage beast who needed taming, he quickly stepped from sight and, on returning into view, wielded a large stick. 'Da said I was to feed you. But seeing as you called me a prick, I don't think you deserve it.'

'Where is your dad? I need to speak with him.'

'He's busy. Now step back.'

Eddie remained where he was, unflinching as Aiden thrashed the air with his stick. 'Get back inside, old man.'

Before Eddie could react, Aiden thwacked Eddie's stomach with the stick, forcing him to his knees, the swift blow taking the wind out of him.

2

It wasn't solely the wedge of afternoon light that stirred Eddie from his dream, but the sound of Jip yelping. It was slight at first, becoming stronger as Eddie regained his senses. He sat up, the stiffness in his bones unyielding. Now on his feet, he staggered to the door and pushed down on the handle. Much to Eddie's surprise, it opened, a burst of cool air filling his lungs as he stepped out onto the grass. The field was bigger than he expected, and after glancing up at the row of ramshackle caravans, he set his gaze on the barbed wire fence and the red brick bungalows beyond it.

Once again, he heard that distinctive yelp. 'Jip,' he cried. 'Jip. Is that you, boy?' The little dog howled in response to his master's voice, causing Eddie to hurry towards the boundary fence. The barking became louder, turning swiftly into a growl, then, at the gruff sound of men's voices, changed to a persistent whining.

Eddie watched the men stroll into view. Paddy led the way. A tan leather overcoat hung loosely over his shoulders, with his oil-stained T-shirt pulled tightly across his gut. He strode with the self-assured gait of a king, and that conniving leech Boyle swaggered alongside him.

Eddie's heart sank when he saw Flynn. The big man's hands were chained, and Paddy's elder son Shaun, and a sly-looking lad, Eddie hadn't seen before, walked either side of him. Young Aiden, holding Jip to his chest, strolled behind, his pasty face veiled in shadow.

On catching sight of Eddie, Shaun looked over his shoulder. 'Ady, you little dick. You were supposed to keep that door locked.' He nodded at Eddie. 'How the hell did he get out?'

Aiden tried to answer, but Paddy spoke over him. 'Ady's had a rough day; he washed and dressed himself this morning, so don't be too hard on him.'

The men howled with laughter, more so as Aiden glared at them. Jip barked in defiance, causing Paddy to flash Aiden an angry look. 'For God's sake, lad, keep that mutt quiet.'

Aiden grunted something in response, then tapped Jip's head, but the fiery little Westie refused to shut up. Paddy nodded at the mean-looking lad standing next to Shaun. 'Michael, you deal with it.'

Michael stood almost as tall as his brother, a detached cruelness settled in his eyes, his short spiky hair emphasised the bushy eyebrows, and the hooked nose matched his pointed chin. He grabbed Jip by the scruff of the neck, holding him at arm's length as the dog growled and snapped.

'You leave him alone,' Eddie cried. He hurried to Jip's aid but struggled to climb over the gate. 'Don't you dare hurt him,' Eddie pleaded while Michael carried Jip back towards the bungalows.

'That's enough, ' Paddy said. He pointed at Eddie. 'No

harm will come to the dog providing you do as you're told. So, keep calm and stop making things worse for yourself.' Paddy walked towards him, took a key from his pocket, and released the chain from the rusty iron gate. The gate swung open with a groan.

Eddie swallowed against the dryness in his throat, the weakness in his knees returning as Paddy and Boyle stood in front of him. Paddy looked over his shoulder. 'Shaun, fetch the big fella. He needs to hear this.'

Flynn was shoved forward, a savage look in his eyes as he and Eddie exchanged glances.

Paddy sighed. 'None of this needed to happen. You two could be lying in your beds now if you'd have kept your noses out.'

Eddie clenched his fists, his fingers aching with arthritis. 'We're only here because of you.' He caught the look of caution in Flynn's eyes. To hell with it, he thought. He had nothing left to lose. 'You give travelling families a bad name. You need to release us, now, all of us, me, Flynn, but most of all, my son.'

Paddy shook his head, smiled. 'You can leave once you've settled your debts.'

'What debts? I don't owe you squat.'

Shaun stepped forward. 'Shall I give him a slap, Da? We can't have him talking like that.'

Paddy shook his head. 'Na. Not yet.' He pointed at the topmost caravan, a windowless rusting heap more derelict than the rest. 'He needs to learn what he owes. Bring out that idiot son of his.'

Eddie felt cold while he watched Shaun shuffle over to the caravan. His shoulders curled forward, his chest caving in as a sour taste filled his mouth. He gazed down at the ground, then looked up, clenching his stomach, feeling the weight of Shaun's every step. Shaun opened the caravan door. 'Come on, boy,' he said as though beckoning a dog. 'Come on, out, don't make me come and fetch you.'

At first sight, the creature who stepped out from the dark bore little resemblance to Trevor. He looked starved and hunched; his hair cropped short, and his sorrowful eyes sank deep into his dirt-smeared skull. Trevor inched forward, reluctant to follow, pausing every few seconds to glance over his shoulder. He drew closer, then stopped, a tearful recognition in his eyes as Eddie called out to him.

'Dad,' Trevor shouted back and ran towards him. The lad covered little ground. Shaun was onto him like a flash, like a predator stalking its quarry; he grabbed Trevor's foot and sent him sprawling, face first, into the grass.

Eddie rushed over to his son, helping him to his feet, and wrapped his arms around him. He kissed the lad's forehead. 'Are you all right, mate? What have these bastards done to you?'

'We *bastards*,' Paddy said, 'have fed that boy of yours and put a roof over his head.'

Eddie gave Trevor a comforting look, then turned to face Paddy. 'That's very good of you.'

Paddy smiled. 'Actually, it is, considering.'

'Considering what?'

'Considering your lad owes me a month's wages. He did half a day then tried to run off.'

Trevor shook his head in denial.

'That's not what you told us before,' Eddie said. 'Liars need a good memory. I don't believe a word that comes out of your ugly mouth.'

Paddy sighed. 'Your belief doesn't change a thing. You and this boy owe us money, and you're going to work it off.'

Eddie shrugged. 'OK, tell me how much and I'll give it to you. Let's get this over with.'

Paddy's eyes narrowed. 'It's not as simple as that. Your lad signed a contract. We paid him up front.'

'Take the money back then.'

Paddy shrugged. 'I would if I could. God knows what he's done with it.' He paused for a second. 'He's staying here until he works it off.'

'We could use them on the Drayden contract,' Boyle interrupted.

Paddy silenced Boyle with a single look. 'Drayden's price is too low. You need to sort that first. Otherwise, stop nagging me about it and shut the hell up.'

Eddie gripped Trevor's hand. 'We're not doing any more work for you. The boy's exhausted. Look at the state of him.'

Paddy grinned. 'He has access to all the amenities. I'm not responsible for his personal hygiene.'

'But you're responsible for him living like a dog.'

'Food and lodgings are provided.' Paddy scanned the other caravans. 'He's treated the same as the rest of the men. I never hear them complaining.'

'I bet you don't,' Eddie said. 'Are they working their debts off too?'

Paddy shook his head. 'Nope. Happy employees, free to leave whenever they want.' He nodded at Shaun. 'I've heard enough from them today. Aiden, get over here and help your brother to get these two idiots back into their caravans.'

3

Flynn had watched in silence, his growing feeling of uselessness reflected by the dejected look on Eddie's face. It was hard to watch: A tearful Eddie desperately trying to hold on to his son as the Finnegan boys dragged him away. Eddie didn't give up without a fight. Even after Shaun head-butted him to the ground, the old man tried to stand. With a bloodied nose, Eddie pushed himself up from the grass. 'Dad,' Trevor called out, but Shaun knocked Eddie back to the ground before he could answer, then stamped his dirty boot across Eddie's face, followed by a swift, hard kick in the ribs.

For a time, Flynn thought Eddie was dead. He felt a surge of fear, followed by relief when the old man started gasping for breath. Shaun dragged Eddie through the grass as though he were a bloodied carcass. Eddie tried protesting, but his body was too weak. With the Finnegan boys distracted, Flynn saw his opportunity. The fools had only bound his hands, so his best chance was to run for it. It seemed cowardly when he thought about it. But for Flynn to get out of here and return with backup was Eddie's only chance.

Flynn darted towards the bungalows, gaining ground until the sound of a gunshot stopped him in his tracks. He slowly turned around, raising his hands at the sight of Paddy aiming at him with a shotgun. Paddy's sons stood behind him, their brazen expressions a marked contrast to the fearful look on Boyle's face.

As though reading Flynn's thoughts, Paddy grinned. 'Go on, big fella. Make a run for it. I dare you. See if I'm a good shot.'

Flynn was in no position to call Paddy's bluff. The intense look in the man's eyes confirmed he would squeeze the trigger without hesitation. Shooting from that range usually resulted in a miss. But knowing Flynn's luck, Paddy would probably hit something, leaving him with a bum leg for the rest of his life. He kept his hands raised, remaining still, concluding he'd run out of chances.

'I knew you were smart,' Paddy said. He scanned Flynn with a wary eye then looked over his shoulder. 'I thought I told you, boys, to tie his legs. This man means us harm.'

Shaun stepped forward and stood alongside his father. 'I need to get another padlock, the one I had rusted up.'

Paddy flashed his son a disappointed look. 'Get it sorted then.'

'I was going to do it later,' Shaun said. 'I did tell you not to let him out.'

Paddy glared at his son. 'You don't tell me anything, boy. He got to see what he needed to.' He turned his face towards Flynn. 'Hopefully, you and that fool friend of yours realise the mess you've gotten yourself into. You need to work that debt off. I'm sure you know the crack when you mess around with the wrong people. It's nothing personal, big fella, just business.'

4

A godawful stench infected the van's interior, a sickly mix of sweat, cigarettes and petrol. Eddie sat with the other men in the line, although looking at the state of the wretched souls, you could barely call them that. Eddie guessed that most of them were half his age. Yet, looking at the stooped shoulders and dispirited look in their eyes, they appeared older. They were an odd assortment. The man seated to Eddie's left stank, his hair, cropped shorter in patches, looked like his barber was a blind man. His clothes were dusty and torn, hanging loosely over his bones, and Eddie wondered if they'd ever fitted him. As Eddie's gaze drifted from face to face, he quickly concluded all these men were of a similar ilk: dishevelled and unfed, their eyes vacant of light, casualties of ill-fated circumstance.

Eddie offered his hand to the bald man sitting opposite. 'The name's Eddie. How long have you been stuck here?'

The man stared down at the floor, the rattle and whine of the van emphasised by the abrupt silence.

'So, where are we headed?' Eddie inquired.

No one spoke; the closest he got to an answer was from the lanky red-haired fellow who squatted by the door, whose sullen eyes, set deep into his freckled face, shot him a warning glance.

It was no mystery to Eddie how these men had gotten to be like this. They were ghosts in a shell, and he feared, especially when he pictured Trevor's face, that he wasn't too far behind them.

After a ride that felt like hours, the van finally stopped. Eddie sat up, the knot in his stomach tightening as the van doors swung open. Michael Finnegan stood smirking in the fierce daylight. A blood-stained bandage covered his left hand, which reminded Eddie of Jip. Michael's glare forced every man to look away. Every man except for Eddie, that was, who held Michael's glare with his own. Michael gestured for him to step outside. 'Come on, quick; Shaun's waiting; we haven't got all day.'

Eddie eased himself up, excruciating pain needling the nape of his back and intermittently stabbing at his hip. Somehow, he managed to stand, although he feared one slight nudge and his knees would give way on him.

A shiver shot through his legs when his feet hit the hard asphalt road. He felt ready to drop, his head muggy with pain, his body yearning for sleep.

Shaun Finnegan grabbed Eddie's arm and herded him onto the pavement. 'Wait there a minute.' Shaun walked back to the van and peered inside. He fell silent, his hands resting on his hips, mouth twitching slightly as though his sluggish brain was trying to think. 'Fox,' he said, and the tall red-haired man stepped outside and stood next to Eddie on the pavement. Shaun looked at them, grimaced, then turned his face towards the van. 'Grills,' he said through a sigh, and the short bald man who had sat opposite Eddie stepped out. Shaun looked at them with contempt. 'Generally, this is a two-man job. But we'll go for two and a half looking at the state of you.'

'Where's my son?' Eddie said. He shot Michael a murderous look. 'What have you done to little Jip?'

Shaun slapped Eddie's face. 'You keep your mouth shut during working hours. Only speak when you're spoken to. And don't talk to my brother like that.'

Eddie forced himself not to answer back, his body couldn't take much more, and the voice in his head pleaded with him to remain silent. It proved a struggle, but thankfully he dealt with it, unsure what was worse, the pain or the humiliation.

From what Eddie could tell, the task set before them was the renovation of a shared driveway. It was a good sixty by thirty feet, which was two days' work at least by Eddie's reckoning.

Shaun put Fox and Grills to work on the Jack Hammers, then handed Eddie a rake. 'You clear up after these boys. Rake and shovel it up into that wheelbarrow, then dump it in the skip.' He stared into Eddie's eyes and grinned. 'And don't get any bright ideas. Trevor isn't working today. He's having a rest. But if you get the notion to speak to someone or run off, we'll get wind of it, and that idiot son of yours won't be so safe.'

Eddie remained silent as Shaun pushed his face closer. 'Are we good with that, old-timer?'

Eddie nodded to show he understood.

Shaun slapped Eddie on the back. 'Good, best get to work then. We'll be back at lunchtime.'

Eddie watched Shaun and Michael swagger back to the van, pretending to look busy until the junk of white metal eventually drove off. Fox and Grills got to work, the machine-gun-like blast of the jack hammers waging war against the day's silence.

Eddie tried to get the men's attention, but they were too absorbed in the task. In normal circumstances, such a work ethic would have been commendable. Today it felt both ugly and strange, two grown men enslaved, their unwavering hard labour driven by fear, as though their captors watched them from a distance, waiting to punish them should they dare to deviate from their task.

Fox and Grills' situation was undeniably bizarre, yet, for Eddie at least, his own felt stranger. All he had to do was walk away and report the Finnegans at the nearest police station. Simple enough when you approached it like that. But with Trevor's life at stake, things were more complicated.

Eddie never doubted the sincerity of Shaun's threat. The Finnegans were leeches who fed off weaker men. He didn't need to go to the police to place Trevor in danger. He'd seen the malice in the Finnegan boys' eyes. One wrong move and they'd kill poor Trev out of spite.

Eddie edged forward with the rake; going through the motions seemed his only option. Maybe Flynn would come good. But in the meantime, Eddie needed this old body to heal and gain the confidence of his compatriots. Strength lay in numbers.

Eddie bided his time. Fox and Grills worked like dogs. Two sweat-laden men, motivated by fear, oblivious to the meaning of rest. After thirty minutes in, they took a break. As Fox removed his jacket, Eddie seized his chance and snatched the dirty rag from Fox's hand. 'Let me put that over here for you.'

Fox answered with a look of wary surprise. Eddie

wondered what alarmed the man more: this selfless act of kindness or the fear that his captors might be watching him. Fox regarded Eddie with a cautious eye, and a half-hearted nod was the closest he came to thanking him. Eddie placed Fox's jacket on the hedge, then turned to face him. 'You've lots of energy; I'll credit you that. For a moment, I thought you guys would never stop.'

Fox looked down at the ground. 'Shaun lets us have a quick break every half hour or so.'

'That's very kind of him,' Eddie said with a sardonic smile. 'Just out of interest, what are these Finnegans paying you?'

Fox and Grills exchanged glances, then Fox said, 'You need to speak with Shaun about that.'

Eddie nodded. 'I thought that might be the case. That's if they're paying you at all. My guess is you're trapped here like the rest of us.' He edged closer and lowered his voice. 'It doesn't have to be like this, you know.'

'It's not *like* anything,' Fox said. 'Be careful what you're saying. Don't let Shaun catch you talking like that.'

'Talking like what? All I'm saying is that there's enough of us to put a stop to it.'

Fox and Grills shared a nervous look. 'You seem like a decent enough fella,' Fox said. 'The best thing you can do to help your son is to keep your head down and just get on with it.'

Eddie stared back in disbelief. 'This is no life.'

Fox shrugged. 'It's the only life we've got.'

Eddie felt a tightness in his chest. 'It's nothing more than slave labour. At least try to leave, for God's sake.'

'Leave to where? Most of us were on the streets before. And even if it was safe to walk out of here, where the hell are we supposed to go? A lot of these men wouldn't last five minutes on their own. Most of them have no family.'

Eddie didn't answer and couldn't quite believe what he was hearing. He observed in silence as Fox limped over to where they'd been digging, Grills following behind him, that dejected look settling back into their eyes as they powered up the Jack Hammers.

The men worked relentlessly throughout the entire morning. Eddie stood and watched, thinking how to get out of this mess while trying to look busy with the rake. The van returned at noon, roaring into the avenue like an unwanted guest, its rusty, battered hulk covered with a film of black dust. Eddie smelled the drink the instant Shaun stepped outside. It drifted through the sweat-tainted air, complimenting the hateful look on Shaun's face. This kid was bad enough when he was sober. Yet the spiteful look in his eyes confirmed he was a meaner drunk.

Shaun raised his arm above his head, and the Jack hammers' deafening roar stopped. He beckoned Fox and Grills closer. They rushed over, two tired old dogs reacting to their master's call. He set a plastic shopping bag at their feet. 'Here's your scran.'

Fox picked it up, opened the bag and handed Grills a cheap-looking bottle of water and an even cheaper looking pack of sandwiches. The men retreated to the hedgerow, wolfing down their food, the smell of egg and mayonnaise carried by the midday breeze.

Shaun turned his attention to Eddie. 'What the hell have you been doing for the last few hours, old man?' He pointed at the debris covering the ground. 'I told you to shift that. The wheelbarrow hasn't budged.' He clutched a pack of sandwiches and crushed them in his hand. 'Everyone earns their keep here. If your work's not up to scratch, then you don't eat.'

Eddie shrugged. 'I'm doing what I can.' He grimaced with pain. 'But if you keep beating a man, he's not going to be much use to you.'

Shaun frowned. 'All this messing around just makes things tougher for little Trevor.' He clicked his fingers at the wheelbarrow. 'If you want to see that idiot son of yours unharmed, then you better get a move on.'

Eddie grabbed the wheelbarrow and wheeled it to the centre of the drive, then started shovelling up the debris, filling the barrow with heaps of soil and stone. He kept his back turned, feeling Shaun's shark eyes burn into him. He went through the motions, slowing his pace when Shaun beckoned Fox and Grills to the van. Eddie watched the men askance, letting the shovel drop from his hands the minute they stepped from sight.

Eddie breathed deeply and took in the view. Except for the distant rush of cars, everywhere was quiet; the neighbouring avenues and streets resigned to the midday hush, people going about their everyday lives, ignorant of each other's plight.

Looking at it from afar, if someone had told Eddie's story to him in the pub, he would have advised a different course of action. Dishing out advice was easy when you were detached. And again, the voice in his head reminded him all he needed to do was walk away. Yet there he remained, ensnared by the love of his son, a sad figure held spellbound by the confines of misfortune.

A shiver passed through Eddie's bones, the ache in his neck intensifying as he glanced over his shoulder.

Shaun clicked his fingers. 'Here. Now. Hurry up, old man. Don't make me say it again.'

Eddie waited for a minute before he strolled over. There wasn't much fight left in his body. But he wasn't a trained dog yet.

Shaun motioned him towards the van. 'Get in.'

Hesitantly, Eddie climbed inside, falling facedown the moment Shaun thrashed the back of his legs with a stick.

5

They dragged Flynn from a dream, where in those brief moments of sleep, he'd wandered through that small Welsh village, then headed to the shore, and it was there that he saw them, the beautiful Nia, a deceitful look in her eyes, standing beside Haines, watching him from those Whistling Sands.

The dream stayed with him all morning, sat hunched and blindfolded in a cold, petrol-tainted van, an immense feeling of loss consuming him. The memory of Nia and Haines's treachery lingered like the stale taste in his mouth. He fought against the rope that bound his hands. God knows what the Finnegans had planned for him. He was sure it was nothing good. He'd seen the defeated look in those men's eyes. For all he knew, Eddie was dead, yet Flynn, with the odds stacked against him, had no intention of being broken.

The van stopped, and minutes later, the doors swung open. 'Out,' said Paddy Finnegan's gruff voice. A hand grabbed Flynn's arm and pulled him forward. Flynn shuffled out, catching a scent of wet grass as the cold air washed across his skin. Paddy removed Flynn's blindfold, grinning while Flynn blinked against the sudden rush of daylight. He slapped Flynn on the back. 'Seems you're going to be famous, big fella. The main attraction. The star of the show.'

Flynn didn't answer. Instead, he looked towards the adjacent field at the cars and vans parked alongside the hedgerows. The men huddled in small groups, collarless dogs roaming freely among them, barking excitedly at the younger boys wrestling in the grass. The men were loud and quick to laughter. Eager to place their bets, growing more boisterous as Paddy marched Flynn closer.

When Flynn entered the field, all heads turned towards him. His presence had a quieting effect. Every pair of eyes appeared loaded with spite.

Paddy whispered in Flynn's ear. 'I'm going to untie your hands now, big fella. So don't go getting any smart ideas. We're all family here. Any trouble from you, and there are plenty of lads around eager to give their rifles a bit of target practice.'

Once the rope slackened and dropped to the ground, Flynn rubbed his wrists. It felt great to have his hands free, but the feeling was short-lived, that sense of dread returning the moment Paddy said, 'Take your coat and your shirt off. I want you stripped down to the waist. Any rings or watches need handing to me.'

Flynn shot him a wary glance. 'What's all this about?'

Paddy scowled. 'Strip down to your waist, I said. Do as you're told; you'll find out soon enough.'

Reluctantly, Flynn took off his coat, hesitating with his shirt when the men started crowding around him.

'Don't be shy now,' someone shouted. 'You best take it off. Ray Calhoun is a beast. He'll rip you and that bloody shirt to shreds.'

Flynn remained silent, slowly removing his shirt as the men roared with laughter.

More men gathered, spreading out to form a wide circle around him. Flynn needed no more explanation. He'd seen enough bare-knuckle fights to brace himself for what was coming next.

The man who stepped into the ring stood well over six feet. He was top-heavy and pale, bare-chested, the flab from his hairy gut hanging over the waist of his faded, dirty jeans. He ran a hand through his greasy hair. A thin layer of dust covered his face.

The man danced on his toes and jabbed the air, unable to mask his smile when the men started cheering. Flynn watched on unimpressed, his eyes fixed on the tall unwashed man who seemed oblivious to his own self-neglect.

A short, stocky man in an off-white shirt entered the ring. He beckoned Flynn and the tall man towards him. 'We want a fair fight, boys,' he said, standing between them. 'No kicking, headbutting or grappling. Just straight boxing. Two-minute rounds until one of you is knocked out or gives up. Now touch hands and give us a good fight.'

The tall man nodded, then pressed his knuckles against Flynn's fists.

The tall man came out fast, swinging wild blows at the air, and almost fell over. Flynn kept his guard, inching forward, unleashing three swift jabs, two to the body and one to the man's face. A look of shock flashed in the tall man's eyes, his chest heaving with every deep breath. He lurched forward in retaliation, his big flabby arms flailing at the air, leaving himself wide open. Flynn followed with his hands and eyes, catching the tall man with a lethal right hook to the face and then another to the side of the head and the tall man collapsed onto his back.

Three men rushed into the circle and lifted the man up, trying to bring him around against the cursing and shouts of disappointment. Flynn wiped the sweat from his brow. 'I thought Calhoun was a killer,' he said to the crowd. 'If I knew it was going to be that easy, I wouldn't have taken my shirt off.'

Roars of laughter sounded their response. 'That wasn't Ray Calhoun,' someone shouted. 'It was Mad McGourty. Thought we'd give you a bit of a warmup.'

Flynn watched in silence as a muscular red-headed man swaggered into the ring. 'Cal-houn, Cal-houn,' the crowd chanted, and Calhoun rewarded their loyalty with a bob and a weave and a few quick punches at the air.

The acting referee beckoned Flynn and Calhoun towards him. 'You both know the rules.' He winked at Calhoun. 'The big fella's tired, so go easy on him.'

Calhoun came out hard, jabbing with his left, looking for the big finish, holding his right hand back. Flynn took his time. Usually, his height and reach gave him an advantage. But Calhoun, although only a few inches taller, seemed to tower over him. To his credit, Calhoun was quick on his feet, continuously poking a straight left at Flynn's face, then stepping back and keeping out of harm's way on the counter. This was the case for the following rounds, and after ten minutes in, neither man had gained the advantage.

Flynn guessed that usually by now, Calhoun had worn his opponent down, weakening them with his jab then achieving glory with that blistering right hand of his. Flynn had other ideas, juking left then right, bringing his hands down whenever he needed to cover himself, weakening

Calhoun with body shots, biding his time for the perfect opportunity.

His chance came in the eighth. Calhoun was already sluggish, his pace slower, his freckled body shining with sweat. Flynn jabbed Calhoun's nose, his knuckles smeared with blood and snot. He saw the worry flash in Calhoun's eyes. But before it could develop into a thought, Flynn smashed a looping right to the head, then smashed his fist into his jaw, and knocked him facedown into the grass.

In their panic and disarray, several men tried to get Calhoun to his feet. But the giant was flat out, the eyes shut tight, and a large wet stain covered his crotch, clear signs that the only place he needed taking to was the hospital.

A grinning Paddy handed Flynn his shirt. 'Get dressed, big fella,' he said, and as the crowd grew more boisterous, Paddy and a few of his compatriots formed a wall in front of him.

Paddy raised his hands. 'Fellas, Fellas, I know you're disappointed and out of pocket.' He looked over his shoulder at Flynn and nodded for him to step forward. Flynn edged closer, tensing his arm as Paddy grabbed it and raised it above his head.

'We have a new champion now,' Paddy shouted. 'Think of the money to be made fellas when we match him against other challengers.'

Flynn tugged his arm free of Paddy's grip, catching the scowls on the men's faces quickly change to half-smiles.

'When's the next fight?' someone shouted.

'Saturday,' Paddy said. 'And then two days after that, and we'll keep going as long as we can. They'll be coming from miles once word gets around. When all the best fighters get wind of Flynn, all of them will want a go at him, and they'll bring their own crowds too, all of them eager to bet.'

'Listen,' Flynn said, 'you can have a better cut if–' He fell silent at the press of cold steel into his back. Paddy spoke softly in Flynn's ear. 'The fella holding the sawn-off behind you will pull the trigger with just a nod from me.' His voice grew harsher. 'You keep your mouth shut, big fella. Do as you're told, and you and that old fool friend of yours might find a way out of this.'

Even a fool could sense Paddy's words were untrue. Flynn needed a way out. As far as he could see, he only had two choices: either die trying or die from exhaustion in an endless fight.

6

Throughout his life, Eddie loathed anyone who mistreated animals. He recalled the time he'd seen a fat drunk kick a dog for no reason. He pictured the poor mutt now, its doleful eyes matching his as he caught sight of his own reflection. Eddie had begged Shaun to stop when he started beating him with a stick. The pain proved too much, and the malice, as seen in Shaun's smile, was relentless. Eddie couldn't move for hours afterwards, and recalling the scene, the tears in his eyes were not from self-pity but a sense of uselessness and shame.

Lying there in that stinking heap they called a caravan, all Eddie could think about was Trevor and Jip. He was desperate to find them, but the weakness in his limbs kept him still, preventing him from turning on his side to protect himself from the cold. Eddie lay there all night, drifting in and out of sleep, the noise of distant traffic washing over him against the relentless hammer of the rain.

The Finnegan brothers came for him a few hours after dawn. They kicked open the caravan door, Shaun watching with his back to the trees, while Aiden and Michael pulled Eddie up by his arms and dragged him into the sunlight.

The air felt warm, laced with the lingering smells of cow dung and newly cut grass. Eddie's legs felt like lead, almost buckling at the knees when Michael shoved him forward.

This time in the van, Eddie followed suit, mimicking his fellow workers by keeping his head down. A flask of coffee and disposable plastic cups made their way down the line. Eddie waited patiently for his turn; he drank slowly, inhaling the aroma and revelling in every mouthful.

The taste of coffee was the closest he'd come to normality in days. Eddie let it loiter inside his mouth; familiar images ran through his mind, then petered out, settling among the distant memories. He wondered if anyone back home had started questioning where he was. Deep down, he knew that wasn't the case; he'd told a few neighbours he was taking a short break, a few days at least, longer if he had the mind to. Eddie shut his eyes and sighed. What a stupid thing to do, but hindsight truly was a wonderful thing.

They dropped him off at a new job–another tarmacked drive. Once again, they partnered him with Fox and Grills. Only this time, Eddie made no attempt at engaging the men in conversation. Instead, he kept himself busy with his shovel and brush, working as much as his frail, old body allowed. Eddie's actions weren't from any sudden change of heart. Fox and Grills were clearly house-trained. Shaun was testing Eddie's resolve, desperate for him to mess up, and the moment he did, Fox and Grills would let him know.

Eddie was no good to his son dead; his biggest fear was whether he would live long enough to help him. He didn't blame Fox and Grills for what they'd done. They had probably been stuck here for years. Duped into believing they were taking free lodgings and a paid job. Days ago, Eddie looked upon the men with sympathy. Now, whenever he caught their gaze, it reminded him of himself–the deadness in their eyes more haunting.

The van returned just after noon. Shaun swaggering towards them, a sureness in his crooked smile as though the world was made to serve him. He handed Fox a plastic carrier bag. 'How's the old troublemaker been today?'

Fox cast Eddie a glance. 'He's been cleaning up.'

'Glad to hear it,' Shaun said. 'Good to see he's finally working.' He pointed at the bag. 'The cheese and pickle are for old Eddie; he needs to keep this up for a few days before he gets a meat sarnie.'

Fox tossed Eddie the pack of sandwiches. Eddie opened it as though he were a ravenous dog, devouring them in only a few bites. He hadn't eaten that way since he was a kid, and the sudden pain in his stomach reminded him how hungry he was. He washed the food down with a bottle of water, sensing Shaun watching him throughout. Eddie didn't look up. He'd wasted enough time being a fool; his cuts and bruises and the constant ache in his bones bore testament to that.

THEY STOPPED WORKING a little after 6 pm. Thankfully, they got rained off. If it had been up to Shaun, he would have kept them going until late evening. The customary defeated silence subdued the journey back. Only this time, Eddie gave in to it. He craved for rest, longing to close his eyes and immerse himself in those quiet hours of sleep.

When they arrived back at the caravan site, Ma Finnegan and her daughter, Aisling, served the men something that resembled a beef stew, each bowl accompanied by a thick slice of stale bread. Eddie took his food without comment, thankful they had finally allowed him to eat. He sat outside his shack, hoping to get sight of Trevor while slurping up the hot juice. There was no sign of his son. Eddie sighed, mopping up the remnants of his stew as he observed the Finnegan women from a distance.

Ma Finnegan was busty and wide-shouldered. Youthful beauty had forsaken her. Now a permanent frown sat across her brow, intensifying as she pushed each fall of dirty-blonde hair from her face. Her daughter, Aisling, stood as her mother had once looked: curvaceous and slim, her big brown eyes wide with youthful expectancy. Anyone could see the two women were related. But it was in the slyness of their smile where they bore the greatest similarity, a look that ran through the entire family. A cruelty Eddie knew all too well.

After the meal, they allowed the men to wash. They passed grey flannels around. Then each man took his turn, cleaning his tired body from a shared washing-up bowl of warm, soapy water. It was a miserable sight, and as Eddie wiped the dirt from his pale, wrinkled skin, he knew he looked the worst of them. They dried themselves with a chequered towel, which was little more than a ragged old dish cloth.

With the men more relaxed, Eddie joined them for a smoke. A hint of pleasure shone in their eyes during this rare moment of quiet contemplation. While Eddie scanned the line, Fox dragged over his chair and sat by Eddie's side. He regarded Eddie for a moment. 'How are you feeling?'

'I'm alive,' Eddie said. 'Well, almost, no thanks to you, seems you're quite the informant.'

Fox glanced down the line at Grills. 'You've got the wrong man. I played no part in that.'

Eddie fixed him with a stare, unsure whether to believe him. He scanned the caravans. 'I thought we all took our break together. Where's Trevor tonight?' Fox met the question with silence, as did all the men when Eddie said, 'Has anyone seen my son?'

Fox shot Eddie a glance, and Eddie watched while Fox's long, nicotine-stained fingers put tobacco on a Rizla and rolled it into a cigarette. He raised it to his mouth and licked the paper's edge, briefly closing his eyes as he lit it up. He took a deep drag. 'I don't know to be honest. He's been on a special job these last few days. Maybe he's still on site.'

Eddie mustered all his strength to calm himself. 'Is he, all right? I haven't seen my boy for days now.'

Fox stared down at the grass. 'He's coping, getting by. The last thing the lad needs is his old man making things worse for him.'

Eddie nodded, the words sounding like something Flynn might have said. Eddie took a deep breath. 'And my buddy, Ned, does anyone know what's happened to him?'

Fox took three deep drags on his cigarette. 'You mean that big tough fella?'

Eddie nodded. 'Yeah, that's the one.'

'They've entered him into the "ring".'

'The ring?'

'Bare-knuckle boxing. They used me for a while till I got hurt real bad. That's how I got this limp. They'll run your friend ragged until he drops. Then when they've no use for him, they'll toss him aside like that dead dog of yours.'

'*Dead dog,*' Eddie said. 'Do you mean little, Jip?'

Fox looked down at the ground. 'Yeah, sorry, I... I didn't mean it to come out like that.'

Eddie clenched his fists and squared up to him. 'Why didn't you tell me before. You should have said something.'

'Shaun told us not to,' Grills shouted down the line. 'He said you'd find out soon enough.'

'I bet he did,' Eddie said. 'Is he responsible for this?'

Fox shook his head. 'It was Michael. He's got a cruel streak in him that one, especially for animals. He's always shooting birds for no reason.'

Eddie closed his eyes for a moment and took a deep breath. 'Did they bury him?'

Fox pointed at the skip placed at the far end of the field. 'Nope. They slung him in that.'

Eddie stood and marched towards the skip, slowing his pace as he drew closer. The smell was unbearable, but when Eddie reluctantly peered inside, it wasn't the bin bags crammed with rotting food that made him sick. They'd placed Jip on an old plasterboard: his tongue lolling out, his little body outstretched. Eddie climbed inside the skip, lifted Jip up, and pressed him against his chest. He held him there for a while before carrying Jip out, and then with tears blinding Eddie's eyes, he lay down with him in the grass.

7

The last three fights were that similar; an exhausted Flynn wondered if he'd been caught in the same never-ending brawl. They'd ordered Trevor to be his cornerman, forcing the lad to towel him down and fetch him water whenever he needed it. Trevor took to his task without objection, an undercurrent of fear driving his enthusiasm. Flynn thanked him every time, casting him a knowing look, doing what little he could to gain the lad's confidence.

As the days progressed, they conversed in whispers. Mostly Trevor pined for his dad. 'Is he all right,' he kept asking. 'When can we go home?'

'Soon,' Flynn always said. Not that he held out much hope. But the lad had been through so much; he deserved someone to console him.

All those blows to the head must have turned Flynn soft. A small part of him didn't want to know. Yet a bigger part had grown fond of Eddie and his boy, and it felt wrong to desert them. The Finnegans needed to get what they deserved. Scum like that hurt people for as long as they could get away with it, although Flynn was determined to break their streak. All he needed was a bit of luck.

Flynn's best chances were at the fights. Word had gotten round, and the new champion quickly gained favour with the crowd. They travelled for miles to watch Flynn fight. Almost everyman slapped him on the back, and those who had made good money were keen for a handshake. It seemed unreal listening to them chant his name. Even Paddy Finnegan looked pleased on the surface, but Flynn saw the greed in his eyes. To Paddy, Flynn was nothing but a prized bull to be hauled off to the abattoir the minute he showed any slack. So far, the fights had been easy wins. But each one took its toll, and as the days progressed, Flynn could feel himself tiring.

Tonight, like every other night, Ma Finnegan, for no one ever called her by her given name, brought his food. She approached him without caution, swinging her hips, a hint of playfulness in those heavily mascaraed eyes. She watched him while he ate, and without fail, after he'd wiped his plate clean, said, 'A man will eat anything when he's starving.'

'I've had worse.'

She smiled teasingly. 'How do you know that wasn't any worse? You've no idea what I've put in that.'

Flynn didn't answer. He refused to think about it. Ma Finnegan, Paddy and their boys were a perfect match. They fed Flynn well compared to the other men. Young Trevor fared the worst; even the dogs had better scraps.

Flynn sensed her watching him as he pushed away his empty plate. She held up a four-pack of cheap lager, placed it beside him. 'Paddy said I was to give you some beer.' She leaned forward and licked her top lip. 'I can share one with you if you like. I've over ten minutes to spare. Paddy's still out. The boys are distracted.'

Flynn shook his head. 'No thanks. I try to stay dry these days.' He gave her body a quick scan. 'And like you said before, I've no idea what's been in that.'

An offended look settled in her eyes. 'Watch how you speak to me, fella. You don't get to say squat. You might well be Paddy's golden boy now.' She snapped her fingers. 'But that can change in a flash if I set my mind to it.'

She glared at him. 'You think you're it, don't you? Enjoy it while it lasts, fella. You'll end up like all those dregs once Paddy has no use for you.' She stared down at the cans. 'That beer will not go to waste. If you won't touch it, then Trevor will. That idiot boy's even more of a clown once he starts drinking.'

Flynn stood up, feeling the chain tighten across his left ankle as he moved away from the wall. At least they'd kept his hands free, restricting his movement to just under three feet, not that any of them dared to come that close. 'I don't think that's a good idea. Trev's not used to the drink; it's not good for him.'

Ma Finnegan stepped back, the cruelness in her eyes deepening as she stood from the safety of the door. She looked over her shoulder towards the main bungalow. 'Michael. Michael,' she screeched. 'Bring that idiot Trevor here.'

Flynn glanced at the ground. 'You don't need to do this.'

Flynn never doubted the validity of her threat. But that wasn't what held him silent. It was the sight of Trevor being led by Michael through the door. Trevor shuffled over to the wall, his eyes large with unease. He shot Flynn a glance as if to ask, what horrors do they have waiting for me?

'We've got you a treat,' Ma Finnegan said as though

reading Trevor's mind. She pointed at the cans. 'Go on, Trev; don't be shy; pick them up.'

Trevor remained still until Michael shoved him forward, following through with a swift, hard kick in the butt. He treated Trevor like a dog, which wasn't a good thing considering the malice he'd shown towards animals. Flynn was tempted to warn Michael off. Instead, he stood silent. Trevor was an easy target, and the last thing Flynn wanted was to make things worse for him.

Michael snatched a can from Trevor's hand, drew back the tab, then pressed it to Trevor's mouth. 'Come on; you heard what Ma said. Drink it.'

Trevor grimaced and shook his head. 'But it tastes horrible. I don't like it.'

Michael slapped Trevor's ear. 'You ungrateful little runt. We paid good money for these. Now get them down your neck.'

Trevor reluctantly took the can from Michael's hand, hesitating for a minute until taking a small sip.

Michael sighed. 'You're testing my patience. Now take a proper swig.'

Tears filled Trevor's eyes. 'I can't. I can't; it makes me sick.'

Michael snatched the can from Trevor's hand. 'You're pathetic.' He pushed it to Trevor's mouth, titling it slightly, forcing him to drink.

Trevor spluttered as the lager trickled down his chin, coughing it back up as he choked. He dropped to his knees, tears spilling down his face. 'Please, Michael,' he pleaded. 'Please, Michael, please, stop.'

Michael grabbed Trevor's shirt. 'Get up, you whining, little maggot. You're disgusting. Get up, I said, before I fetch the stick.'

'Enough,' Flynn shouted. 'Leave the poor boy alone.'

'All this is your fault,' Ma Finnegan said. 'If you'd have drunk those cans, none of this would have happened. Beer costs money. If you won't drink it, then Trevor will.' She looked at Trevor and shook her head in disgust. 'Down to the last drop. Now get up.'

As Trevor stood, Flynn pointed at the cans. 'Pass them here. Let's get this over with.'

Ma Finnegan nodded at her son. 'Give him the cans.'

'I think Trevor should finish them.'

She gave Michael a furious look. 'Don't make me ask you again, lad, or Trevor won't be the only one heading for the stick.'

Without further protest, Michael did as he was told. He nudged the remaining cans towards Flynn, then hastily stepped back to a safe distance.

Flynn glanced down at the cans. 'I'll drink them later. Why not let Trevor get cleaned up first?'

Ma Finnegan forced a laugh. 'You'll drink them now where I can see you. How stupid do you think I am?'

Flynn answered her with a look, picked up a can and pulled the tab open. He winced at the sudden smell of beer, a smell that took him back to bleaker times. Images of the Whistling Sands flashed through his mind's eye, the sea dark and cruel, as those dull, alcohol-fuelled days blended into one.

As the warm, cheap lager ran down his throat, Flynn wondered if he'd been deluding himself all along. All his attempts at staying dry were nothing but self-delusion. Like his father before him, the drink was in his blood; why try to avoid the inevitable? At least this time, it was for a good cause. Poor Trevor had suffered enough. Flynn had let

Eddie down. Returning to the drink was the least he could do. It was hardly the greatest of sacrifices.

A look of triumph gleamed in Ma Finnegan's eyes while she watched Flynn finish the last can. 'I knew you were an Alky. You've got that look, gagging for more now, are you? I can see it all over your face.' She looked across at Trevor. 'Put those cans in the bin; then make yourself scarce; I'm sick of seeing your ugly face. Straight to your caravan, mind. No dawdling, I'll be watching you.'

Trevor took to his task, peeking up at Flynn as a way of thanks. When he was done, he rushed outside. Flynn watched until the lad's gaunt figure vanished into the evening's dwindling light. Then he focused on Ma Finnegan while she slowly stepped closer. 'You've got a taste for it now, huh?'

Flynn didn't answer.

'Course you have, Alkies are all the same. I've half a bottle of whisky in the house. You can finish it if you like.'

'No Ma,' Michael said, 'Da told us–'

'Shut it, boy. You mind your own business and go and fetch the bottle from the house.'

'There's no need,' Flynn said.

'Sure,' Ma Finnegan scoffed. 'Michael, fetch it all the same. Let's see how reluctant he is once he's had a whiff.'

Michael shook his head. 'No. I'm not having anything to do with this. Da wants him clean for the fights.'

'Whatever,' Ma Finnegan said. 'I'll go fetch it myself.' She hesitated by the door and spoke at Flynn over her shoulder. 'A bit of whisky won't harm a big fella like this. Anyway, according to him, he won't touch a drop.'

Once he was alone, Flynn closed his eyes in dismay. He felt useless chained here like a dog. This was the perfect and perhaps his sole opportunity with Paddy and Shaun away.

He pulled savagely at the chain, then, as he tired, slid down to the floor, leaning his head into his hands.

Ten minutes later, Ma Finnegan returned holding a half-empty bottle of whisky. Flynn noticed she'd brushed her hair, sprayed herself with perfume. All her efforts were in vain. Even if she was the most beautiful woman in the world, that spiteful smile ruined her looks.

She offered Flynn the bottle, stepping back after he yanked it from her hand. He put the bottle lip to his mouth, overstating his pleasure with every swig.

Ma Finnegan flashed him a smile. 'You're enjoying that, I can tell.'

Flynn opened his eyes. 'Yeah, it's been a while. Shame to drink it on my own, though. If that offer still stands. Why don't you join me?'

She hesitated for a moment, then moved closer with an exaggerated sway of the hips. She looked different this close, a hint of youth in her smile, the meanness in her eyes softening. Flynn offered her the bottle, grabbing her arm with his free hand when she reached out for it. He tightened his grip, watching the frantic look in her eyes as she tried to pull away. Flynn let the bottle smash on the floor and placed his arm around her neck.

He pressed his mouth to her ear. 'Do you think I'm going to share a bottle with an evil, cold-hearted bitch like you?' He could hear her heart thumping. 'Drink just makes me mean. But you're too stupid to see that.' Flynn loosened his hold slightly, knowing what she would do.

'Michael, Michael,' she yelled. 'Go fetch your Da. The brute's got hold of me.'

8
___

A woman hollered, and a young man's voice cried out in reply. Eddie opened his eyes, his body rigid with cold, realising all the fuss was coming from the main bungalow. The noise was enough to rouse the dead. He pushed himself up, carried Jip's little body to the hedge, and concealed it in the tall grass. He stared down at it for a moment, then started walking in the direction of the main bungalows.

Some of the men came outside, but none got too close. Like tamed creatures, they observed from the safety of their caravans.

Breathless, Eddie stopped when he reached the gate. He leaned his weight against it, watching as Michael and his sister ran across the lighted courtyard. The girl held a baseball bat while her brother carried a shotgun over his shoulder. Eddie eased open the gate, keeping close to the exit.

Much to Eddie's delight, Flynn had his arm around Ma Finnegan's throat. 'Unlock these chains,' Flynn said coolly. 'Or I'll break your mother's neck.'

'Do as he says,' Ma Finnegan shouted, although young

Michael was having none of it. He aimed the shotgun at Flynn. 'Leave, Ma alone or I'll blow your head right off your shoulders.'

Flynn stepped to his left, ensuring Ma Finnegan stood directly in front of him. 'Do your worst. Let's hope for your mother's sake that you're an amazing shot.'

Even though Eddie could only see Michael from behind, it was enough to know that he was locked in a state of nervous indecision by the tightness of the lad's shoulders. Eddie wanted to kill him, sneak up on him with a stone and smash his warped brains out. Something held him back, weariness, old age, or the dread of messing up.

'Put the gun down,' Ma Finnegan said. 'Throw him the keys, then fetch your father.'

Michael lowered the shotgun. 'Da's got the keys.'

Eddie watched as Flynn tightened his grip.

'Now's not the time to get smart, lad,' shouted Ma Finnegan. 'You know there's a spare set by the kitchen window.'

Michael shrugged. 'Don't know which one it is.'

Ma Finnegan glared at her son. 'It's the only brass key there, lad. You know that. Stop playing the fool.' She closed her eyes and sighed. 'Aisling, fetch it before your idiot brother gets me killed.'

The girl followed her mother's instructions without protest. Yet before she reached the door, Paddy's Land Rover, followed by Shaun's van, came hurtling through the gate, filling the yard with dust.

Paddy stepped out from the Land Rover and slammed the door shut behind him. Eddie moved closer to the wall, anxious in case Shaun, who now stood by his father's side, caught sight of him. Paddy shot Michael a glance, then stared into the bungalow.

'The big fella's got Ma,' Shaun said, though before he could go charging in, Paddy held him back. 'Stay put. Let me deal with it.'

Paddy moved closer, stopping a few feet away from the bungalow. He stared at his wife, who stood helplessly in the doorway. 'What's all this about?' Paddy said. 'For God's sake, woman, what the hell have you gotten yourself into.'

'He–' Ma Finnegan tried to explain, but before she could say another word, Paddy silenced her.

'You keep your mouth shut, woman.' Paddy released a sigh. 'What's all this about, Flynn? What do you expect to gain from it?'

'I thought that was obvious. You pass the key. Then fetch Eddie and his boy, and we'll be out of here.'

Paddy grinned. 'You know I can't do that. It's personal now. It's passed beyond paying a debt. That old man bears too much of a grudge. I need to protect my family.'

Flynn tightened his hold around Ma Finnegan's neck. 'You can do that now. Just give me the key, and I swear I won't harm her.'

Paddy shook his head, smiled. 'I'm not convinced you will either way.'

'Don't be too sure about that. You know nothing about me.'

Paddy grinned. 'That's where you're mistaken. I've been asking around. I know more about you than you think. I reckon I've got you sussed.'

'Bullshit. You know nothing about me.'

'I know you did time with a man called Jack Meadows. He said you're dangerous enough. But you've got a good heart. That's a weakness for men like you. He said once someone got into your head, you're a soft touch.'

'Jack Meadows tells folk what they like to hear. He'll spin you any yarn if you give him enough drink.'

Paddy grinned. 'I read people pretty well. He convinced me, told me all about Mason and his wife. Love makes you do strange things. A man must have a big heart to kill for a woman like that.'

'Just rumours.'

'Is that right,' Paddy said. 'The thing with rumours is they tend to stick.' Paddy turned his back on Flynn and walked over to Shaun. 'Fetch Trevor, let's put an end to this.' He turned to face Flynn. 'Let's test that big heart of yours.'

'It's your loss, Paddy. It wouldn't take much to break your wife's neck.'

Paddy shrugged. 'Suit yourself. You'd be doing me a favour to tell you the truth. That woman's nothing but trouble.' He scowled at his wife. 'How the hell did she get herself into this mess. She's got a roaming eye, that one. The bitch probably came on to you, no doubt.'

When Shaun returned dragging Trevor by the arm, Paddy turned to meet them. He beckoned Trevor closer, and when the lad reluctantly stepped forward, Paddy put his arm around his shoulder. 'Are you all right, Trevor?' he said gently.

Trevor nodded.

'Are you sure, now?'

Trevor nodded again, almost causing Eddie to come from his place of hiding and shout out to him.

'That's good to hear,' Paddy said. 'You remember that feeling because you'll need it afterwards.'

Paddy held his smile as he took off his belt. He wrapped the buckle end around his fist, allowing enough of the tail to use as a lash. He struck the air, then satisfied it was fit for purpose, he whipped the side of Trevor's head with two fierce resounding slaps.

Trevor fell to the ground. 'Please, no, please,' he kept shouting as Paddy laid into him.

Eddie rushed to his son's aid as swiftly as his body allowed. He pushed Paddy aside, then knelt in front of Trevor to shield him. Trevor wouldn't stop shaking, and Eddie stared in silence at the wet patch around the lad's crotch. He gripped Trevor's hand. 'Shush now, son. Dad's here,' he said, trying to comfort him.

'Get this old fool out of the way,' Paddy said. And no sooner had Eddie glanced up than Shaun grabbed his shoulders and started dragging him across the yard. The sharp edges of the stones scraped across Eddie's skin, but the pain was nothing compared to the heart-breaking cries from his son.

Eddie could do little, even less so when a hard kick to the chest winded him. With tears in his eyes, Eddie watched from the confines of his sudden paralysis, saddened and ashamed as Paddy continued to beat his son.

After every lash, Paddy looked at Flynn. 'Let her go, Flynn, or I'll beat this boy to death. Just let her go; it doesn't have to end like this.'

From where he lay, Eddie could just about see Flynn standing behind Ma Finnegan in the doorway. He saw Flynn tighten his hold of her. Yet when Trevor continued to cry out, Flynn loosened his grip. Eddie, filled with an immediate sense of both relief and defeat, closed his eyes.

Now released, a pale and dishevelled looking Ma Finnegan spat in Flynn's face. 'You'll regret this,' she said and, avoiding her husband's glare, marched across the yard. Only her daughter appeared concerned, linking her mother's arm with her own as she guided her back to the main bungalow.

Flynn braced himself as Michael and Shaun moved towards him.

'Stay put,' Paddy ordered. 'He's got a fight in the morning. I'm not losing money because of you two.'

Shaun wore a look of disbelief. 'You can't let him get away with that.'

Paddy didn't reply, but the look he gave his eldest son was enough to silence him. He stared down at Trevor. 'Take this lad back to his caravan and give him something nice to eat.'

Shaun nodded towards Eddie. 'What about that one?'

'Let Mikey take him. Check on the others. I don't want anyone else getting funny ideas and lock all the caravans.'

Paddy's sons exchanged glances and then took to their tasks with a slow shrug. Michael ordered Eddie to stand, but when Eddie struggled to get to his feet, he grabbed Eddie's shoulders and tried pulling him up.

'All right, all right,' Eddie said, 'give me time for God's sake.' It took a lot of effort to push himself up from the ground. He felt unsteady on his feet, every slow step riddled with pain, and it was difficult to stop himself shaking. Despite this, he walked, stopping to catch his breath when they came to the gate. Trevor waited near the wall, and on seeing Eddie, hurried over and stood by his side. Trevor put his hand on Eddie's shoulder. 'Are you OK, Dad?'

Eddie reassured his son with a smile. 'I'm fine, mate. It'll take more than that to finish me off.'

Shaun pushed his way between them. He stank of sweat, and as he said, 'Come on, shift,' Eddie got a waft of stale beer from his breath.

Eddie took hold of Trevor's hand and squeezed it as hard

as he could. 'We're coming. But I'm walking back with my son.' He shot Shaun a fierce look. Who knows what Shaun saw in Eddie's eyes? Whatever it was, it seemed enough to allow Eddie and Trevor to stay by each other's side during the slow walk back.

After passing through the gate, Eddie paused and glanced over his shoulder. He could see Flynn's outline watching from the doorway. His face was obscured by shadow, and, for the first time since they met, the big man's hunched figure looked so much smaller.

9

A familiar hint of triumph glowed in Paddy's eyes, a look that Flynn was growing tired of. As Paddy stepped closer, Flynn stood up. 'You better bring your best fight to me, Paddy, because I can assure you it'll be your last.'

Paddy smiled. 'Now, why would I do that on my own? Even after today's debacle, you still think I'm an idiot.' He took out his pipe, occasionally glancing up at Flynn as he loaded it with tobacco. He struck a match against the wall, turning the yellow flame around the surface of the pipe bowl, his face becoming redder with every puff.

Appearing satisfied the pipe was lit, Paddy took a deep drag, filling the doorway with a fog of grey smoke. He plucked the pipe from his mouth and pointed the stem at Flynn. 'This happens when you go soft, big fella; folk like me get the better of you.'

Flynn frowned. 'I'm not going soft.'

Paddy grinned. 'Really?'

'Yes, really. And you haven't got the better of me. But you can tell yourself what you like.'

Paddy took two more puffs on his pipe. 'You say that as if I'm deluded.' He glanced down at Flynn's chains. 'A tad stupid, don't you think, for a man in your situation.'

Flynn couldn't disagree. He felt pathetic standing there, open, vulnerable, an easy target for the vagaries of lesser men.

Paddy, maintaining a safe distance, went and stood by the opposite wall. 'I don't think this would have happened a few years ago.' He puffed twice on his pipe. 'No, I imagine the Flynn of old would have snapped that bitch's neck without a qualm. Even if he couldn't escape. He would have done it out of spite. To be honest, the Flynn of old wouldn't have gotten himself into this mess in the first place.' He watched Flynn with a half-smile. 'That's what happens when people make their problems yours. They muddy the mind. Slow you down. The weak and needy are leeches, Ned. Give them the slightest chance, and they'll suck the life from you.'

'I don't see anyone doing that to you, Paddy. It's the other way around, from what I can see. If anyone's having the life sucked from them, it's the men you've got locked up in those caravans.'

'Bums and wasters. Their own life choices brought them here, Ned. Granted, the boys are rough with them at times. But without this place, those men would be on the streets, drugged and pissed up, getting up to God knows what.'

'If you're so sure, then why not let them go?'

'Most of those men are on contracts.'

'And those who aren't?'

'They can leave whenever they want.'

'And what about our contracts? You must have got your money back by now, especially from my fights, three times over?'

'Yes, if things had run smoothly. But you and that old man have caused nothing but problems. It's gone beyond contracts now, Ned. It's complicated, and you just made it personal. No doubt that whore came on to you, but she's still the kids' mother, and you threatened her life for God's sake.'

'I did. You should call the police.'

'*Police*,' Paddy scoffed. 'Is that the best you can come up with? You know I won't do that. It's not what you want either. The thing is, Ned, you need to have a long hard think. You've used up all your options. You're not going anywhere unless I say so.' Paddy glanced over his shoulder. 'That old man's on his way out, and that idiot son of his is no use to anyone. Do yourself a favour and drop any ideas about helping them. They'll end up getting you killed. You don't strike me as a fool, Ned. Look at the trouble they've brought you so far. It's downhill all the way with them two. It doesn't take a genius to see that.'

Flynn bowed his head and stared down at the ground, then looked up towards the sound of Paddy's laughter.

'It's hard to argue against, isn't it, Ned?'

Flynn remained silent. All he wanted at this moment was to wipe the smug look off Paddy's face. He took a deep breath. 'And what if I was to forget about the old man and his son? What are you offering that's any better? What's in it for me?'

Paddy glanced around the room. 'I can get you out of this dump for a start. Put you in one of the nicer bungalows; bring you women too.'

'Letting me go would help.'

Paddy smiled. 'I know it would. That's a discussion we can have later, perhaps. Now we have an issue of trust.' He stared into his pipe, 'blasted thing,' he muttered, then tapped the bowl a few times against the wall, letting the burnt tobacco fall to the floor. 'Trust makes everything run smoothly, Ned. But we can work on that.' He made his way outside, stopping at the door as his daughter, Aisling, strode towards him.

'Boyle's on the phone, Da. He needs to speak to you.'

'Tell him I'll call him back.'

Aisling sighed. 'He's been calling all morning, says it's urgent.'

'It's nothing that can't wait. Tell him the Drayden contract's fine, providing they up the price.'

Aisling mumbled something beneath her breath then stormed off.

Paddy turned around to face Flynn. '*Boyle*. Now there's another loser for you.' He shot Flynn a smile. 'You'd do well to think about what I've said. It's an excellent offer if you ask me, and from where I'm standing, you don't appear to have that many options.'

'What about my share of the money you make from those fights?'

Paddy grinned. 'Now that's more like it. Trust, Ned. Trust. You gain that, and anything's possible.'

10

The night sky shone bright, yet the shabby confines of the caravan remained wretched even when bathed in moonlight. A shiver ran down Eddie's spine at the thought of leaving Trevor alone. So far, all his attempts had failed. He'd ruined any chance of trying to win the other men's favour, and the only option now was to get help, an impossible task, considering how the Finnegan boys watched him like a hawk. But it was pointless trying to sit things out.

Eddie stood up, ignoring his fear and apprehension and that persistent dull ache. On their father's order, the Finnegan boys now ensured the caravan door remained locked. It hadn't occurred to them to check inside. Most would have struggled to climb out through the small window, especially a frail old man.

Fortunately for Eddie, no one had noticed the severe rust near the disused sink. Why should they? The caravan smelled too bad to venture inside, and except for the stained mattress they made Eddie sleep on, old boxes cluttered the interior.

When removing one of those boxes to create more space, Eddie noticed a huge wet stain on the floor. On closer inspection, he discovered they had replaced part of the original flooring with plasterboard. Over the years, water from the leaking pipe had soaked through. It was mouldy and rotten, so much so that Eddie had managed to push his fist through. These last few days, he'd lacked the energy to make the hole wider. But tonight, he felt invigorated by desperation.

At first, Eddie loosened the plasterboard with his hands, and when it started proving more difficult, he tried kicking it through. He did this in brief spells for fear of bringing attention to himself. When the hole could grow no wider, Eddie stepped back. A child would barely squeeze through. Eddie knew this from the start. It was the reason he'd held off for so long. He stared down at the hole, then sat down on a box.

After ten minutes of silence, Eddie gave it another try. It wasn't as though he had much choice; the alternatives didn't bear thinking about. He knelt, gripped the jagged edges of the hole, and pulled the plasterboard towards him. It wasn't until his fourth attempt that it shifted. The rusty screws budged, causing Eddie to pull harder, and that feeling of hopelessness, which dogged his waking hours, faded as the board split. It came easier after that, Eddie ripping the board away as though it were paper.

The exposed layer of plastic sheeting stank of damp and mould, Eddie stamped down on it, piercing it with the heel of his shoe. He felt his heart thump inside his throat, more so as he caught glimpses of the grass. Eddie ripped the sheeting apart, then lay face down on the partly covered ground. For a moment, he feared it was all a dream, but the notion quickly passed, its reality confirmed by the night air falling coolly across his skin.

Eddie breathed deeply, his body stiffening, held rigid by a sudden feeling of claustrophobia. He gritted his teeth and, using his stomach to propel himself, crawled sideways like a crab.

Lying on his stomach, Eddie took in the neighbouring fields and the glow of lights from the distant bungalows. The wet grass seeped through his clothes, and on forcing himself from the ground, he almost slipped. He skulked behind the caravans, stopping when he drew closer to the trees.

Part of him wanted to go back for Trevor, but the lad's caravan would be locked, and with this being his only opportunity, it wasn't worth the risk. So, with a heavy heart, Eddie stepped into the woods. At a guess, the road was about a mile and a half away. He planned to cut across through the trees, and that's what he did, mindful not to fall, groping his way through the darkness.

The intermittent sounds of passing cars grew closer as he gained more ground. Eddie quickened his pace, encouraged by the flashes of headlights. Eventually, the trees tapered off onto a broad gravel path. Eddie followed it, stopping when he came to the road. He reckoned his best bet was to head south. Hopefully, he would come across a village or a town. A car passed him without stopping, even though he tried flagging it down.

'To hell with you,' he shouted at its dwindling lights. Not that he could blame them. Who in their right mind would stop for a deranged, tattered old man? Eddie glanced up at the sky. Clouds shrouded the moon, and the only protest against the night's silence was the tired sound of his every breath.

Eddie stood still when the vehicle drove slowly towards him, then held up a hand to shield his eyes against the dazzling headlights. The driver's dark silhouette shifted in his seat. Eddie stepped closer, looking over his shoulder when another vehicle pulled up behind him. Both engines died; the headlights dipped, and when Eddie stared into Shaun Finnegan's contemptuous eyes, he felt a lump in his throat, his heart thudding dully in his chest as the van doors swung open.

11

The Finnegan boys kicked open the door and carried Eddie in. Shaun gripped Eddie's arms while Michael held his legs. 'We've brought you some company,' Shaun said through a grin. Then the brothers tossed the old man on the floor as though they were disposing of an old carcass.

When the Finnegan brothers departed, Flynn got up and crouched by Eddie's side. 'What the hell happened to you? Are you all right?'

Without opening his eyes, Eddie slowly shook his head. 'No, I'm not,' he said in a frail voice. He touched his ribs, raising his head an inch to sit up.

Flynn stared at the blood trickling from Eddie's nose and mouth. The old man's trousers were dusty and torn, his left eye almost swollen shut and his hands covered in scrapes and cuts. 'Looks like they really went to town on you.'

Eddie managed a weak smile. 'Tried to get help. Almost made it...' he broke into a cough.

'Try to rest, Eddie. I'll fetch you some water.'

When Flynn returned, he held the bottle to Eddie's mouth. 'Here, try and take a sip.'

A frazzled-looking Eddie didn't reply, and when he showed little sign of movement, Flynn put his hand behind Eddie's head to help him sit up.

'No,' Eddie groaned. 'Let me lie here for a while. I'll be all right in a bit.'

Flynn nodded and went back over to his mattress, the chain dragging behind him. He studied Eddie with a watchful eye, calling out his name whenever the old man appeared to stop breathing.

'I'm all right,' Eddie said with a sigh. 'You're getting soft in your old age. Fretting over me like that. Didn't you advise me once to only care about number one?'

Flynn smiled. 'Don't you go thinking otherwise. I only asked if you were all right.'

Eddie's laugh broke into a breathless cough. Flynn rushed over to his side. 'Do you need to sit up?'

Eddie shook his head. 'No. I'm better on my back; apparently, it helps clear the airways.' He shot Flynn a sad look. 'I'm sorry, Ned.'

'For what?'

'Dragging you into this mess.'

'You didn't drag me into anything. I came looking for you, remember. We made a deal. No one put a gun to my head.'

Eddie sighed. 'I've made a pig's ear of everything.'

'Don't talk like that, Eddie. You did what you could to help your son. Hell, I wish I'd have had a father like you.'

'He was a piece of shit, huh?'

'That's an understatement.'

Eddie nodded and closed his eyes. 'I asked about him. A

nasty man by all accounts. A few said you were a chip off the old block.'

Flynn stared down at his bruised knuckles. 'Maybe I am. It sure as hell explains everything.'

'Maybe,' Eddie said. 'But my father taught me we're accountable for our own actions. We can't always blame someone else for the things we've done.'

Flynn didn't respond, and in the silence that followed, observed Eddie with a watchful eye.

The old man didn't look well. His face was a pale grey, and the occasional rattling sound from his chest had turned into constant wheezing.

Flynn stood up and walked towards the door.

'Where are you going?' Eddie said in a hoarse voice.

Flynn glanced over his shoulder. 'You don't look good, Eddie. I need to get their attention. They need to take you to the hospital.'

Eddie slowly lifted his hand. 'No, Flynn. Leave it alone, please. You know what they're like. It'll only make things worse.'

Flynn conceded with a sigh. He walked over to Eddie and sat beside him. 'I expect you're right. The best you can do is try to rest.' Flynn stared into the old man's sad eyes then looked away. He could sense Eddie staring, but before he could ask him what was wrong, Eddie said, 'Believe me, Ned. She's not worth it.'

'Who isn't?' Flynn said, feigning ignorance.

'That woman you're searching for. The one who's driven you crazy.'

'*Crazy?*'

'Yeah. She must have to drag you into all this mess. You need to forget about her and move on.'

'It's not as simple as that, Eddie. You don't know what

she's done.' Flynn paused. 'What would you do to the Finnegan's if you had half a chance?'

The answer flashed in Eddie's eyes.

'Exactly,' Flynn said. 'You can't forgive some things.' The image of Nia's smile lingered in Flynn's mind. He closed his eyes for a moment, suppressing any more thought of her, burying them deep with all the other dark memories.

'North London,' Eddie said.

Flynn gave him a bewildered look.

'That's where that Cresswell fella is.'

'Who told you that?'

'Someone I know who used to work in the Liverpool passport office.' Eddie stopped to catch his breath. 'They're self-employed now. Bespoke passports if you get my drift.' He shut his eyes and winced. 'That Cresswell fella ordered three.'

Flynn moved closer. 'How long ago was this?'

'A couple of weeks ago.'

'He'll be out of the country by now.'

Eddie shook his head. 'I doubt it. Ordered, not received. It takes time to make a convincing fake, and the last I heard, they were quarrelling over price, probably still waiting.'

'Where?'

'North London. Harinley, I think?'

'Harringay.'

'Aye, that sounds about right.'

'And who's this friend of yours?'

'A man called Stan Linden.'

'Lives close to you?'

Eddie shook his head. 'He's down south too. Harrow Road.' Eddie paused. 'Not that it does you any good. Not stuck in this godforsaken place. But a deal's a deal. You kept your part of it. You could have...'

As Eddie broke into a cough, Flynn helped him sit up, using the cuff of his jacket to wipe the bile from Eddie's chin.

'You didn't need to do that,' Eddie said with a hint of shame in his voice.

Flynn took off his jacket and placed it by his side. 'Can't let you lie there like a dribbling old man.'

Tears pooled in Eddie's eyes.

'I was only–'

'I know you were,' Eddie said. 'I just feel so bloody useless.' He released a defeated sigh. 'I wish I could see my lad. It would break his mam's heart if she saw us like this.' Eddie fell silent, his tears getting the better of him.

'Hey, stop that. Try not to upset yourself, Eddie. All you need to do now is rest.'

Eddie gripped Flynn's hand, clutching it tighter as he vomited on his chest.

'Let me clean that up,' Flynn said. He reached for his jacket and wiped it away. 'And don't you worry about anything, Eddie. We're going to get out of here, me, you, and Trevor. All we need to do is–'

Eddie's hand went limp. Flynn looked up at Eddie, and even though the old man's eyes were still open, Flynn knew his friend was gone.

PART III

1

Flynn called out to them for hours, but no one came until noon. Paddy didn't have the decency to show his face. Instead, he sent his two younger sons, Aiden and Michael. Aiden appeared unable to look at Eddie head-on. The lad kept slipping his hands in and out of his pockets, observing the old man's body through sidelong glances. Michael was less apprehensive. His eyes glowed as he stared down at Eddie's body, his open shotgun resting on his shoulder. He turned towards Flynn. 'Da said we're to take the old man's body to the bottom field, so you and his idiot son can bury him.'

Flynn glared at him. 'Eddie deserves a proper funeral. You need to call someone.'

Michael rolled his eyes. 'Sure. Who do you have in mind?'

'An ambulance would be a good start. Eddie needs to be in a chapel of rest, then we need to arrange a proper funeral.'

Michael shook his head and let out an ugly laugh. 'As if we're going to do that. Shall we call the police too?' His smile faded, and a callous look settled in his eyes. 'Aiden, wake up Trevor and bring him here, and grab some dust sheets from the van.'

Flynn stepped forward. 'You can't let his boy see him like that.'

Michael closed his gun and pointed it at Flynn. 'We'll do as Da says. If you're so upset about this old fool, you can join him.' He glanced down at the chain, then stepped back as if suddenly acknowledging that it was the only thing that prevented Flynn from taking a run at him.

Flynn considered how to draw the boy closer, but before he could give it any thought, Paddy came swaggering in. Shaun followed behind, each man carrying a shovel on their shoulder.

Paddy rested his shovel against the wall and, turning to Michael, said, 'Stop waving that thing around like it's a toy. One dead man's enough.' He turned his face to Flynn. 'Sorry about your friend. Shaun got carried away. But that's the risk you take when you have your own agenda.' He gave Eddie's body a scathing glance. 'Crazy old fool bust a hole through my property. I'm passing the debt onto you. A few more fights should pay for it.' He plucked a small set of keys from his pocket and threw them at Flynn's feet. 'You can't dig a hole chained up.' He snatched the gun from Michael's hands. 'And don't try anything stupid, Ned. I'm handy with this. I've shot quicker and smaller things than you.'

Paddy glared at Michael. 'I thought I told you to cover the body up.'

Michael's eyes narrowed. 'I am if you give me half a chance, Da. Ady's gone to fetch a dust sheet.'

'I told *you* to get Trevor. Someone needs to carry that body out.'

No sooner had Paddy mentioned Trevor's name than the

lad, escorted by Aiden, stepped shyly into the bungalow. On catching sight of his father's body, Trevor's face paled. Flynn knew, if he were fortunate enough to survive this place, the look of disbelief and despair captured in the boy's eyes would haunt him for years to come.

Trevor stood and stared; tears burned in his eyes, and his body, still at first, shook, more so as the horror set in. 'Dad... Dad,' he cried, running towards Eddie's body, stopping when Shaun blocked his way.

Shaun gripped Trevor's arms. 'Easy now. You calm yourself.'

'Dad... Dad.' Trevor shouted. He looked towards Flynn. 'What's wrong with him, Ned? Why won't he answer me?'

'Because he's dead, you idiot,' Michael said with a wide grin. 'And if you don't stop blubbering, you'll end up the same way.'

Trevor tried to free himself from Shaun's grip, but he proved too strong for him. He kicked Shaun hard in the shin. 'You little shit,' Shaun said and grabbed Trevor in a headlock.

Flynn quickly unlocked his chain and stepped forward. 'Leave him alone. The lad's grieving, for God's sake.'

Paddy pointed the gun at Flynn's chest. 'Stay where you are, big fella. He'll have plenty of time to grieve once we've buried him.' He shot Aiden a fierce look. 'Cover the man, for Christ's sake. We're not animals.'

Aiden did as he was told and spread the dust sheet over Eddie's body. Paddy looked at Shaun. 'Let him go; he needs to help with his father.'

Flynn rolled up his sleeves. 'You shouldn't force him to do that, not in his state.'

Paddy shrugged. 'Fine. You can do it on your own then. You can carry him on your shoulder.'

'Carry Dad to where?' Trevor asked, now free from Shaun's grip. He edged over to where Eddie lay and knelt by his father's side. 'Carry Dad to *where*?' he said again. 'Ambulance needs to come now. Dad's friends need to sort the funeral.'

An expression of disbelief settled over Trevor's face, and he fell silent as he lifted Eddie's hand and pressed it to his cheek. As the lad broke into a sob, Flynn walked over to him. 'Come on, Trev. Your dad wouldn't want to see you like this.'

Flynn rested a hand on his shoulder. 'Come on, Trev,' he said, but the lad was inconsolable. Flynn turned towards Paddy, who answered with a nonchalant shrug. 'What are you looking at me for, Ned? I told you what you need to do.'

Flynn closed his eyes for a moment. He crouched over Eddie's body. 'We need to bury your dad.'

Trevor shook his head, refusing to budge. 'No. Not here. Not in this place.'

Paddy released a long, exasperated sigh. 'You don't have any choice, boy. We're not having a rotting corpse lying around.' He gestured towards Shaun. 'Move him aside. Ady, grab those shovels. Let's get this done. I haven't got all day.'

With a cold and unfeeling look in his eyes, Shaun grabbed Trevor and dragged him towards the door. Trevor did his best to put up a fight, but when Michael came to his brother's aid, the Finnegan boys proved too strong for him. They dragged him out to the courtyard, ordering him to shut up, slapping the side of his head whenever he cried out.

There was little Flynn could do. So, with a heavy heart, he lifted Eddie's shrouded body from the dusty, concrete floor and carried it on his shoulder.

2

Flynn stood on the wet gravelled courtyard, staring towards the Finnegan's bungalow as he shifted the weight of Eddie's body across his shoulder. Ma Finnegan watched him from the kitchen window, her dishevelled blonde hair falling across the side of her face, partially covering her black eye. Flynn held her stare with his own, averting his gaze the instant she flashed him her cruel grin. He sauntered towards the field while Paddy trailed behind him with his gun.

In the distance, he could see Michael and Aiden, and behind them, Trevor's stooped figure wading through the wet grass. A few of the men watched sheepishly from their caravans. Their presence made Flynn realise it was a Sunday. Even the damned got time off.

As Flynn and the others reached the bottom field, Michael waited for them at the gate. He swung it open to let them through and, looking at Paddy, said, 'Aiden's with Trevor at the far end.'

Paddy fixed him with a stare. 'Tell Trevor to start

digging. I want this thing done. I'm in no mood to stand in this blasted rain all day.'

As Michael ran ahead, Flynn slowed his pace, mindful of the wet grass, and with Trevor now in view, the last thing he wanted was for the boy to see him slip. Much to his relief, he carried Eddie's body the rest of the way without incident. He lay it down carefully by the hedge, and no sooner had he caught his breath than Paddy ordered him to 'dig.'

Flynn snatched the shovel from Michael's hand and thrust it into the patch of earth near to where Trevor had dug. He cast Trevor a glance and, in a lowered voice, said, 'Just keep your head down and throw yourself into it. You follow my lead, and it'll be over sooner than you think.'

The soil was hard and stony, and after thirty minutes in, they'd made little headway. Flynn dug faster, more so for Trevor's sake, ignoring Paddy and Shaun's demands that they get a move on.

The rain fell harder, and as they lifted every spadeful of soil, the mound of earth at their side rapidly turned into mud. Flynn stopped to wipe the rain from his eyes, each breath feeling heavier than the last. His arms ached, his legs weakening, and as he stretched, he felt the sweat trickling down his back. 'How deep do you want this?' he said without looking up.

'Six foot,' Paddy said.

Flynn slammed the shovel into the soil. 'Four's more realistic.'

Paddy sighed. 'Get on with it then. The way you're shifting, we'll be lucky if we get two.'

Flynn and Trevor exchanged glances. A coldness had settled in the lad's eyes. Flynn had seen that look before in other men. 'Are you, all right?' he said in a half-whisper. Trevor didn't answer. Instead, he dug faster, Flynn matching his speed, both men, from the outside at least, appearing resolute in completing their task.

As the hole grew deeper, so did the ache in Flynn's back. He felt the stiffness in his bones, and Trevor looked fit to drop. 'Slow down a bit,' Flynn said, but with a determined shake of the head, the lad refused to stop.

They had about a foot and a half to go by Flynn's reckoning. But the earth was rockier now, and it took all their strength to get the larger stones out. Flynn's hands shook as he lifted one from the ground, the wet soil making it harder to get a good grip.

Flynn's tired arms could barely hold the weight, and as he dropped the stone on the muddied mound, he almost trapped his fingers. Flynn stared down at his hands. His nails were black with dirt, and smears of dried blood marked his fingers. Trevor looked worse. The lad looked more creature than man, soaked to the skin, pale and emaciated. His sunken eyes stared blankly ahead. His hair, flattened by the rain, stressed the shape of his skull.

Flynn tapped the lad's shoulder. 'Stop for a while.'

Trevor shook his head. 'No,' he said with a weak breathy voice. 'Can't leave Dad in the rain. We need to bury him.'

Flynn couldn't disagree. But as the exhaustion kicked in, he feared Eddie wouldn't be the only one laid to rest. He slammed his shovel in the ground and leaned into it. Paddy and his sons stood by the fence, taking shelter beneath the trees. Paddy pointed at Flynn with his gun. 'Get that hole dug.'

Flynn was too tired to answer back, and Paddy, as though responding to the haggard look in Flynn's eyes, said, 'Get him buried. Then you'll have plenty of time to rest.'

Flynn glanced over his shoulder at the sound of someone moving through the grass. It was Paddy's daughter,

Aisling, the permanent scowl she wore looking more agitated as she marched begrudgingly through the rain. She headed straight for Paddy, shoulder-barging Shaun on her way past.

In retaliation, Shaun gave her a shove. 'Jesus, girl. What's wrong with you. What the hell did you do that for?'

She gave him a fierce look. 'That Ian Boyle has been calling you for the last hour. You left your phone in the house. I'm not your personal secretary.'

Shaun glared at her. 'Never said you were, girl. You didn't need to come out here just for that.'

Aisling rolled her eyes. 'He kept pestering, said it was important.'

Shaun spat into the grass. 'If Ian Boyle's involved, then it's nothing that can't wait.'

Aisling rested her hands on her hips. 'I told him to leave a message. But he kept ringing, insisting it was important.' She threw Paddy a glance. 'He said it would piss Da off if I didn't tell him straightaway.'

Paddy scowled. 'Tell me what, girl?'

Aisling wiped the rain from her face. 'Something about the Draton contract?'

'Drayden,' Paddy corrected her.

'Yeah, that's the one.'

'What about it?'

'He said it's about to go "tits up". Tell your Shaun and your dad that they need to speak to them and sort the price, or the brothers are going to walk.'

Paddy grimaced. 'That Boyle is a waste of space.' He shot Shaun a fierce look. 'I warned you not to involve him.'

'He's been fine until now,' Shaun protested.

'No, he hasn't,' Paddy said, shouting him down. 'You're always wiping his arse. It always surprises me how the man gets himself out of bed in the morning. Aisling, did you bring Shaun's phone with you?'

Aisling shook her head.

'For God's sake, girl.'

'Don't have a go at me. I didn't have to traipse here in the rain, you know.' She glanced down at Eddie's body, then at Trevor, averting her gaze when Flynn caught her stare with his.

Paddy conceded with a nod. 'No, I know. We'll come back with you to the house.'

He handed the gun to Michael. 'You and Aiden keep an eye on these two until we get back.'

Aiden straightened his shoulders, losing that thousand-yard stare as though Paddy's words had suddenly woken him up. 'What if they give us any trouble?'

Paddy flashed Flynn and Trevor a smile. 'You'll be fine, Ady. The only thing you need to worry about is that they bury the old man before they drop.'

3

Flynn watched Paddy, Shaun, and Aisling until they were nothing more than three dark specks fading into the distant fog. Michael looked in his element, holding the gun, while all Aiden seemed to care about was keeping dry from the rain. Flynn and Trevor shared a glance, and when the lad continued to dig, Flynn edged closer. 'Don't work too hard,' he whispered. 'Try to preserve some energy.'

Trevor didn't reply. Instead, he continued to dig, occasionally stopping to stare at Michael. Flynn picked up his pace, hoping to get the old man buried before he and the lad collapsed.

Ten minutes later, Flynn rested his shovel on his shoulder and called out, 'We're done.'

Michael stepped out from beneath the trees. 'Da said six feet.'

'We agreed four,' Flynn said. He glanced down at the ground. 'This trench is deeper than that. It's more than enough.'

Michael frowned. 'More than enough for what?'

Flynn scrubbed his hand over his face. 'To bury him. But I suppose you need your dad's permission before we do that.'

Michael straightened. 'I don't need his permission for anything.'

Flynn nodded. 'Let's bury him then. None of us wants to stay out in the rain.'

Michael pointed the gun at Flynn. 'What are you waiting for? And don't try anything, or we'll bury all three of you.'

Flynn climbed out from the makeshift open grave and offered Trevor his hand. The lad gripped Flynn's forearm, weighing next to nothing as Flynn pulled him out. They walked over to Eddie and lifted him off the grass, the soaked dust sheet covering the old man's body like a second skin. They carried him to the open grave and lowered him in.

Fate had a perverse sense of humour. It was hard to believe that a few months ago, Eddie was at home enjoying his retirement. Eddie was all too aware of the evil folk were capable of. But he would have jeered at the thought of what life had planned for him. Yet the reality remained all too real. A stark, undeniable truth that chilled Flynn like the rain.

Flynn and Trevor began filling the grave, starting slowly, then gaining momentum once they'd covered the body. Judging by the speed at which Trevor moved, it was hard to imagine that thirty minutes ago, he was close to collapsing. He shovelled the soil like a man possessed, mumbling to himself while he worked. His soaked clothes hung heavily from his raw-boned frame; his dark, deep-set eyes glistened in the fading light.

When they'd finished, Trevor stood gasping for air, tears rolling down his cheeks.

'Let's head back,' Michael said, and when neither man

replied, he grew more insistent. 'Let's go back. Now. Don't make me ask again.'

'Hey,' Flynn said, edging closer.

Michael aimed the gun at Flynn's head. 'Stop where you are. Now. Turn around and take your friend back to the house.'

Resting the shovel on his shoulder, Flynn made an open palm gesture with his free hand. 'Take it easy. We don't want any trouble. But the lad has just buried his father, for God's sake. We need to say a few kind words before we leave. It's the least we can do.'

Michael sneered. 'I'll give you a few words. Here lies a stupid old fu–' Before he could say another word, Flynn slammed the shovel into his face.

Michael stumbled back towards the trees, his face smeared with soil and blood. He fumbled with his gun, but before he could squeeze the trigger, Flynn stabbed the edge of the shovel down onto the lad's shaking hands. Michael's eyes widened with fear and shock as though he couldn't believe what was happening. Flynn struck him again, then another to the side of the head, missing the third blow as Michael dropped.

Michael lay bloodied and still, but when Flynn bent down to pick up the gun, he noticed the lad was still breathing. He rummaged through the lad's pockets and grabbed the remaining cartridges, then, as he looked up, caught sight of Aiden sprinting towards the bungalows.

Flynn threw Trevor a glance. 'You all right?' he said, then pointed towards the trees. 'The safest way out of here is through these woods. We need to move fast. Do you think you can manage that?'

Trevor responded with an unconvincing nod. He stared down at his father's grave then stepped towards Flynn. The gusto and drive, which had accompanied him several minutes ago, appeared to have deserted him.

'Are you sure you're all right?' Flynn said.

'Yeah,' Trevor said, looking ready to drop.

'OK. Follow me and bring your shovel; you're going to need it.'

Flynn led them to the trees, constantly looking over his shoulder to ensure Trevor was still behind him. They ventured deeper into the woods, hurrying their pace as the roar of a car engine drew closer. Flynn looked over his shoulder and peered through the trees, catching glimpses of Shaun's van speeding through the grass. There was no sign of Paddy's Land Rover; Flynn guessed that he'd driven to the far end of the woods to cut them off at the road. He glanced at Trevor and sighed. 'Except for the road and where we came in, is there another way out of this place?'

Trevor stared at him blankly. 'I've never been here before.' He looked up at the surrounding trees. 'What are we going to do, Ned?'

Flynn shrugged. 'Make our way towards the road, try to get there before they do.'

'And if we don't?'

'Hunker down, I guess. Our best bet is to draw them in.' Flynn saw the fear settle in Trevor's eyes. 'You swing that shovel at anyone and anything that tries to hurt you. Do you hear me?'

Trevor nodded.

'Good, lad, stay alive and stay safe. Don't hesitate; just lash out. You can think about it later.'

4

The rain had eased, the air thick with the smell of wet soil, and a half-moon, breaking through the clouds, partly lit the sky. They advanced in silence. Flynn led the way, inching forward, alerted by the rustle of every leaf, the dull beat of his heart, and whenever a twig snapped. He kept the gun closed. All shots needed to count, and with only a few cartridges, there would be no second chances.

As they neared the edge of the woods, Flynn signalled for them to stop. He stood silently in the thinning trees, listening to the sound of distant traffic and the heaviness of his breath. From the headlights of a passing car, he glimpsed Paddy's Land Rover. 'Get down,' he whispered, and both he and Trevor rested on their haunches. He saw two figures move towards the trees, and from behind him came the sound of someone treading carefully through the woods. A dog barked in the distance, and the distinct sound of Shaun's voice called out to it.

Flynn looked at Trevor and pointed westward. 'You

move as fast as you can. Find somewhere to hide, and don't come out until I say.'

Trevor answered with a nod, gripping his shovel close to his chest before fleeing into the trees.

'I've spotted the runt, Da,' Shaun shouted. 'You and Ady come in close. I'll set the dogs on him.'

The barking faded off into the distance and no sooner had Flynn stood up than the sound of gunshot ripped into the air like thunder.

Flynn fell to the ground.

'I've dropped the big fella,' Shaun yelled wildly.

Flynn checked his body for blood, but thankfully, he wasn't hit.

Flynn felt his heart beating inside his throat, squeezing his eyes shut as he considered his options. Instinct told him to move, belly-crawl through the leaves and hide in a safe spot. Yet the voice inside his head forced him to stay put, let them come to him. Running scared would only get him killed. If he could get one of them down, it would improve his chances.

He sensed Shaun draw closer, could smell him, that familiar mix of alcohol and sweat. Flynn gripped his gun, standing the instant Shaun stepped into sight, and squeezed the trigger, blasting Shaun's shoulder.

Shaun stared at the wound open-mouthed. His eyes widened with shock. 'Da, Da,' he wailed. But before he could say another word, Flynn rammed the butt of the gun in his face. He heard his teeth crack. Blood spewed from the lad's nose as he fell on his ass. Flynn motioned to strike him again, pausing as Shaun rolled on his side, bent his knees close to his chest, and shielded his face with his hand. 'No, please. No,' he whimpered.

Flynn picked up Shaun's pistol. A foul smell filled the air, and Flynn stared at the brown runny stain oozing through the seat of Shaun's jeans. Flynn shook his head in disgust, and before reloading the gun, gave him a swift kick in the ribs. 'Get up and put your hands behind your head.'

'I can't move,' Shaun whined. 'My shoulder's in bits.'

'Up or that shoulder will be the least of your problems.'

Shaun didn't move, forcing Flynn to grab him by the collar and drag him to his knees. 'Put your hands behind your head.'

Slowly lifting his left arm, Shaun did as he was told. His right arm remained by his side, dangling like a slack rope. 'And the other one,' Flynn said.

'I can't move it.'

Shaun flinched as Flynn pressed the muzzle into the back of his head. 'Do you have any more cartridges?' Shaun didn't answer; he just stared straight ahead at Paddy standing among the trees. Aiden stood by his father's side, stunned, the fear and shock in Shaun's eyes mirrored by his own.

Paddy held his rifle against his chest. 'Move away, big fella. You've already left one of my boys half dead. I won't let you make it two.'

Flynn shoved Shaun's head with the tip of his gun. 'You're in no position to give orders. Just throw me your keys and step back.'

Paddy narrowed his eyes. 'You think you're just going to drive out of here after what you've done.'

It was odd to see Paddy taking the moral high ground. For a moment, Flynn was lost for words. He shook his head in disbelief. 'You killed an innocent man, buried him in your field, for God's sake.'

Paddy raised the rifle and pointed it in Flynn's direction. 'Yeah, well.' He stared down the barrel. 'I guess some people deserve what they–'

Once Paddy squeezed the trigger, Flynn plunged to his left and fired back. Both men missed, and while Paddy took cover in the trees, trying to reload, Shaun scrambled clumsily to his feet and dashed towards a darkened patch in the woods. Aiden ran off too, scampering towards the road like a frightened rabbit in the moonlight.

Paddy backed away, firing another shot as Flynn chased after him. Paddy might have been a coward, but he was no fool. Heading back to the Land Rover was his best choice, and if he got back on the road, he would gain the advantage. Flynn reloaded then jogged through the trees, closing in, taking cover whenever Paddy fired a shot.

Every shadow looked like a man's shape, waiting, watching in the half-darkness. Flynn heard a noise and, turning to his left, saw Shaun hobbling across a clearing in the trees. He was breathing thickly, and on catching sight of Flynn, pointing the gun at him, he fell to his knees. 'I'm asking you, begging you. Please, Flynn, no good will come of this.'

Flynn moved closer. 'You should have thought about that when you beat Eddie to death.'

'You've got it all wrong. Da was the one who went too far. I just do what he tells me.'

'Did he tell you to beat Trevor whenever you felt like it?'

Tears filled Shaun's eyes. 'Just take me to the Land Rover. Da will cut you a deal. As long as I'm alive, he'll let you drive away.'

'We've already tried that. Paddy doesn't care about you. I had a gun to your head, and he still shot at me.'

Shaun hung his head, his shoulders shaking while he cried like a baby.

'Get up,' Flynn said, almost tempted to put the scumbag out of his misery.

Shaun got to his feet and slumped back against a tree. The frightened look in Shaun's eyes reminded Flynn of Trevor. He only hoped the boy had found a safe place to hide, and if he had any sense, he'd stay put.

Flynn wanted to call out to him. Even he wasn't that stupid. The last thing he wanted was to give Paddy the advantage. Paddy had either gotten back to the road or waited for him in the trees. Either way, if Flynn moved forward, he'd be an easy target. His best option was to backtrack to the field and get to Shaun's van.

Flynn clicked his fingers at Shaun. 'Toss me your keys.'

Shaun dug frantically into his back pocket and threw the keys in Flynn's direction, a bullet skimming across the side of Flynn's face the moment he reached out his hand.

It felt as though someone had set fire to Flynn's cheek, the cut less than an inch from his eye. Another shot followed but went wide, resonating among the silent trees. Disoriented from the first shot, Flynn crouched down. Shaken and in pain, he tried to focus, yet no sooner had he got his bearings than he heard a shrill whistling sound followed by fierce barking. Something approached him from behind and as he turned his head, one of Shaun's dogs, returning from the hunt, snarled then bit into his shoulder.

'Kill him, Rex,' Shaun cried. 'Hurt him, boy. Da, Da Rex's got him. Quick Da. Quick, while he's still on the ground.'

Flynn didn't respond. He was too busy grappling with the dog, pounding it in the ribs, then sending it off whimpering into the woods after landing two heavy blows to the poor thing's jaw. Blood seeped through Flynn's shirt. Droolladen bites pierced his arms and fingers. He pushed his hands into the ground, a sudden kick in the face forcing him onto his back.

Flynn was out for a few seconds and on opening his eyes, Paddy, as though he were the grim reaper, stood over him. He kicked Flynn in the groin, then stamped on his hands. 'Bastard,' he said through gritted teeth, every curse followed by a quick hard kick in the ribs.

Flynn rolled onto his side and rested on all fours, inching through the leaves as Shaun's grating laughter chased after him. Shaun rested his boot on Flynn's back. 'Where the hell do you think you're going? Give me the gun, Da. Da, Give me the gun.'

Paddy shook his head.

'He had me on my knees. Give me the gun, Da. Let me finish him.'

Paddy looked at Flynn and smiled. 'The sacrifices you make for your children. I can't deny my boys a thing.'

Flynn knelt upright. If he were going to take his last breath, he would face it head-on. He fixed Paddy with a defiant stare, catching glimpses of the blurred shape bobbing and weaving between the trees, then stood up the instant Trevor's scrawny figure stepped into the moonlight.

In the seconds before Trevor swung the end of the shovel into Paddy's jaw, Paddy stared at the lad as though he was a ghost. Paddy fumbled for his gun. Yet Trevor, to his credit, was too quick for him. He struck Paddy to the ground, slamming the shovel end against his skull, over and over, until Paddy lay motionless. Shaun tried to intervene, but Flynn, landing a solid punch to his injured shoulder, soon put a stop to that.

Flynn took the shovel from Trevor's hands. 'Let's go,' he said softly.

Trevor didn't respond, and Flynn followed the lad's gaze to Paddy's bruised and bloodied face. 'Let's go,' Flynn said again, raising his voice over Shaun's sobbing.

Flynn grabbed Trevor's arm. 'It's done with, Trev. Let's go home now.'

5

They headed back to the end field, walking side by side in silence. When they got to Eddie's grave, Trevor stopped. He stared at it for a moment, tears streaming down his cheeks, took a deep breath and shot Flynn a doleful glance. 'I'm not leaving Dad here.'

Flynn nodded. 'In normal circumstances, I'd agree–'

'Let's call people.'

'No, Trev. That means telling the police.' Flynn glanced towards the woods. 'We can't do that. I'll sort it. I promise. But for now, we need to get the hell out of here.'

Trevor shook his head.

Flynn sighed. 'There's a dead man in those woods. One laying wounded, and another one, possibly on his last breath. The last thing we need is the police. They wouldn't take much convincing that I'm to blame for all this.'

'I don't care. I want to bury Dad properly. Dad always said, "if you do something wrong, you need to face the consequences."'

Flynn rested a hand on Trevor's shoulder. 'You've suffered enough. All your dad cared about was your safety.

He wouldn't want this. We'll bury him properly. I promise. But let's get you home first. We've spent enough time in this godforsaken place.'

From the look in Trevor's eyes, something about Flynn's words seemed to persuade him. He answered with a hesitant nod and went with Flynn to the van, remaining silent as he walked beside him.

Flynn drove slowly up the field, flicking the headlights to full beam, glancing at the line of pale men and their yapping dogs, watching him from outside the caravans. Holding a dog on a leash, a tall red-headed man stood by the open gate. Flynn beeped him to move out the way. When the man refused to budge, Flynn took a deep breath and glanced at Trevor. 'Who the hell's this joker?'

'Fox,' Trevor said. 'He's all right.'

Flynn stopped the van and grabbed the gun. 'For his sake, he better be.' He wound down the window. 'Do you have a problem, friend?'

Fox shook his head.

'Good, get out of the way then.'

Fox nodded towards the woods. 'Where's Paddy and his boys? Shaun told us to follow him with the rest of the dogs. We heard gunshots.'

Flynn scowled at the yapping dog. 'Paddy and Shaun are indisposed. Aiden's hiding in the trees. Do you have a problem with that? Or have you come to finish the fight?'

Fox shook his head. 'No,' he said and spat on the ground. 'Paddy got what he deserved. Good riddance to bad rubbish if you ask me.' He glanced over his shoulder towards the main bungalow. 'Ma Finnegan and her daughter might disagree, though. Michael's in a bad way.'

'They called the police? An ambulance?'

Fox shook his head. 'Nah, not with all these men here. Too much to lose. Even they aren't that stupid.'

'They've called no one?'

'I never said that. Paddy comes from a big family.' He gestured towards the van. 'I wouldn't travel in this if I were you, especially around these parts. It sticks out like a sore thumb.'

Flynn frowned. 'You'd rather we walked?'

Fox shook his head and stepped aside. 'I never said that, was just trying to–'

'We should go in Dad's camper van,' Trevor said. 'I've seen it parked up in the courtyard.'

'We need to go, Trev. Now's not the time for this.'

Trevor opened the passenger door and jumped out. Flynn slammed his hand down on the steering wheel. 'Get back in, for God's sake. We need to get out of this place.'

Trevor shook his head. 'We're going back in Dad's van.' He marched towards the bungalow. 'It's all I've got left of him.'

Flynn killed the engine, jumped out of the van, and raced after him. He grabbed Trevor's shoulders and turned him around. 'This is stupid. You're going to get us both killed. Don't you think we've been through enough?'

Trevor nodded at the camper van parked alongside the garages. 'There it is,' he said, his voice becoming more excited.

Flynn took a deep breath. 'It's probably out of petrol. We don't even have the key.'

Trevor freed himself from Flynn's grip. 'There's a spare under the mat. Where Jip used to sit.' He dashed over to the van and swung open the passenger door, dropping to the ground as the roar of a gunshot tore into the night sky.

Ma Finnegan stepped into view, holding a shotgun, her

hair, wild like the look in her eyes, shining beneath the fiery hues of the driveway light. 'I've got a dying son in the house. You responsible for that?'

Flynn inched forward, staring down at Trevor, who lay lifeless on the ground.

'Stay where you are,' Ma Finnegan said. She pointed the gun at Trevor. 'Or simple boy here will end up the same way, and this time I won't miss.'

Flynn nodded. 'Are you all right, Trev?'

'Yes,' he said weakly.

'Good, lad. Stay where you are; we'll be out of here soon enough.'

Ma Finnegan pointed the gun at Flynn. 'You're staying here until Paddy's brothers arrive.' Her voice quivered at the mention of Paddy's name. 'I take it Paddy isn't coming back?'

Flynn nodded. 'There's no need for this to get any worse. We've all suffered enough.'

Ma Finnegan's shoulders stiffened. 'Paddy's brothers will be the judge of that.'

Her fierce glare faded as she looked towards the far end of the courtyard. Flynn turned around and saw the men from the caravans, led by Fox, walking towards them.

'Stay back,' Ma Finnegan yelled. 'I'm warning you.'

The men moved forward, forming a circle around Fox as he pressed himself towards the gun.

A look of uncertainty flashed in her eyes. 'Get back,' she warned. 'I'll blast his guts out, then drop every one of you.'

Fox snatched the gun from Ma Finnegan's hands. 'How are you going to do that with one shot.'

'Don't talk to me like that.'

'Or you'll do what?' Fox said.

Ma Finnegan, backing up towards the door, didn't answer.

Flynn gestured for Trevor to stand, but the lad was already up. Trevor rummaged inside Eddie's van, and thirty seconds later, he showed Flynn the key. Flynn took it from his hand. 'Get in, Trev,' he said, then jumped in the driver's seat.

Flynn slotted the key into the ignition. The damn thing wouldn't start at first, but after a few more frantic twists, the engine roared throatily into life. Flynn shifted into first, staring at the men's ghostlike faces watching him as he reversed down the driveway. He backed slowly onto the road, checked for oncoming traffic, then turned right.

THEY'D BEEN DRIVING for at least fifteen minutes before Flynn caught his breath. He drove as fast as the van allowed, which, even on the flat stretches of road, never exceed sixty. Flynn pushed open the glove compartment, fumbling inside for a mint, surprised to find an old pack of cigarettes. He popped one in his mouth, taking deep drags as he held the car lighter to its tip.

Trevor pushed the smoke away.

'Sorry,' Flynn said.

Trevor flashed him a weak smile. 'That's OK. I like the smell. It reminds me of Dad, from long ago, when he used to smoke.'

Trevor sat back and closed his eyes, his breathing growing heavier as he drifted into sleep.

It felt as though, driving through the quietness of the night, the horror they'd left behind was nothing but a bad dream. But Flynn knew that wasn't the case. Every passing car reminded him it was true, the headlights beam illuminating his mud-caked hands and the smears of blood across Trevor's gaunt face.

THANKS FOR READING

Thanks for reading. If you **enjoyed this book,** please consider leaving **a review**. Reviews make a huge difference in helping new readers find the book.

Check out the first book in the Ned Flynn Series
THE WHISTLING SANDS

WITCHES COPSE - AVAILABLE FOR PRE-ORDER

Redemption Comes at a High Price...

It's 1979, the Winter of Discontent, and gun for hire, Elizabeth Daton's career ends abruptly when a job results in a young girl being hospitalized. Her luck changes when renowned barrister, Quentin Quinby hires her to travel to a remote Welsh village and escort an acquaintance of his back to London from the ominous *Witches Copse*.

Daton agrees, desperate to make amends, believing she's been given a second chance. But what begins as a simple errand quickly escalates into a terrifying ordeal of possession, witchcraft, and the occult. Can Daton triumph or is she doomed to pay redemption's price?

ALSO BY MATH BIRD

Veteran conman, Nash returns to his hometown to locate the money stolen from him. All he has is a hunch and a newspaper clipping of the boy who witnessed his partner's death. Their fates become entwined, but in a world of violent drifters and treacherous thieves, a man's conscience can become his weakness.

A poignant and dark thriller, rich with atmosphere, for fans of small-town crime and rural noir.

Praise for WELCOME TO HOLYHELL

"Welcome To HolyHell has the sharp plotting of peak Elmore Leonard combined with the brooding lyrical atmosphere of James Lee Burke. The characters are all marvelously well-drawn and the sense of time and place is spot on." *Punk Noir Magazine*

"Math Bird gives us a fine bit of noir in 1976 Wales." *Murder in Common Crime Fiction Blog*

"A remarkable work that will have you dreading as well as eagerly turning the page." *Unlawful Acts - Crime Fiction blog*

ALSO BY MATH BIRD

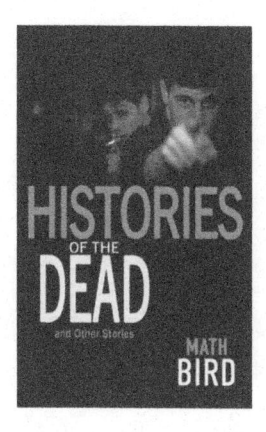

A beautiful collection of hauntingly dark crime stories.

West of the River Dee, lie the borderlands of north-east Wales, an in-between place caught between two countries.

Travel inland and you'll pass through the towns and villages, where ancient relics and abandoned factories harbour the ghosts of past glories. The tree-clad hills snake up from the valley where secrets and dark deeds whisper through the tall trees.

Whether they are fearful of the future, or worried that their best years are behind them, the characters of this striking short story collection are haunted by the past; they live on the periphery, because sometimes to live, love, or just survive, vengeance is the only option.

ABOUT THE AUTHOR

Math Bird is a British novelist and short story writer.

He's a member of the Crime Writers Association, and his work has aired on BBC Radio 4, BBC Radio Wales, and BBC Radio 4 Extra.

For more information:
www.mathbird.uk

Made in the USA
Las Vegas, NV
11 January 2022